ANDREW STRONG

OSWALD AND THE END OF THE WORLD

SCHOLASTIC

First published in 2007 by Scholastic Children's Books
An imprint of Scholastic Ltd
Euston House, 24 Eversholt Street
London, NW1 1DB, UK
Registered office: Westfield Road, Southam, Warwickshire, CV47 0RA
SCHOLASTIC and associated logos are trademarks and or registered trademarks
of Scholastic Inc.

10 digit ISBN 1 407 10258 3
13 digit ISBN 978 1 407 10258 0

British Library Cataloguing-in-Publication Data
A CIP catalogue record for this book is available from the British Library

Printed by CPI Bookmarque, Croydon, Surrey
Papers used by Scholastic Children's Books are made from wood
grown in sustainable forests.

1 3 5 7 9 10 8 6 4 2

www.scholastic.co.uk/zone

Thanks to

Mother Fortune
Jackie Head (bless your antennae)
Catherine Clarke (agent extraordinaire)
Elv Moody (impossibly talented, dream editor)
Ellie, Jake and Mary (for lovingly guiding me
through the real world)

also
espresso, oulipo, Glenn Gould's piano
(near perfection)

ONE

What a way to die, swallowed whole by a sea creature.

After all I've been through I don't expect a gentle exit from this life. But to be swallowed whole is a bit much.

Here it comes, passing beneath us; I can see its long shadow lurking below as we tread water. Dad doesn't know it's there, and is trying to decide which way to swim, hoping that Mother Fortune will send us a sign. He's scratching his chin, almost as if he can't make up his mind what we should do with the rest of the morning. I don't want to break the bad news to him – the creature has already worked it out.

The sky behind us is brightening. At least we get to see the beginning of a new day, even if it is our last.

I take a look at the world. It is so perfect and untarnished, just sea, sky and fluffy clouds. So unlike the string of grim islands we've trudged across recently, desperately trying to make a living.

We haven't eaten properly for a month, haven't slept under a roof for longer. On the island of Greater Fury we were left with nothing but a cormorant's egg to sustain us, and a piece of old sailcloth for shelter.

"Don't you worry, boy," Dad puffed last night, as we ran down the pebbles, dragging a tiny, stolen fishing boat into the surf. "They don't call me Mercurio the Marvellous for nothing!"

Who did he mean by "they"? "They" certainly aren't the sour-faced miseries who chased us off Greater Fury into the sea, their fists hammering the air and their dogs howling.

And nobody on any of the other forsaken islands called him "Mercurio", or "Marvellous". More like "liar", "cheat", "rogue" and "thief". Back on the mainland, when he named himself "Wonderful Walter, the Man with the Magical Hands", he was called far worse things.

When the boat heaved and shook last night, throwing us out into the water, Dad thought it was just a freak wave, a bit of bad luck. I know the truth; I saw the sea creature's huge, dark shape.

Dad bobs about, looking up, still waiting for a sign.

"Mother Fortune!" he yells. "Which way now?" He looks from cloud to cloud, swivelling in the water. He wants Mother Fortune to point the way home. Suddenly he perks up.

High above us, silhouetted against the brightening sky, is a lone seabird.

"An eagle, Oswald! Look!" he splutters, kicking into the water next to me. "A majestic bird. It is a good omen. We're almost home and dry."

It isn't an eagle, it isn't anything like an eagle. It isn't big enough. But details like this never worry Dad. It looks more like a seagull, and like us, it's probably lost.

Across the water I can see the distant flicker of lights on Mardy End island and beyond, further out to sea, the beam of Craven Lighthouse sweeping the waves, still visible in the dawn light.

"Mardy End, Dad," I croak, not sure how much longer I can keep afloat. "Please. Let's just swim towards Mardy End."

But he isn't listening to me. It's the voice of Mother Fortune that beckons him.

"She's telling us we must follow the eagle!" he yells.

In the last few weeks he's got so much worse, one minute believing he can see the future in tea leaves or in a slug trail across a stone, the next telling me that we need to talk about Mum, about how much we miss her. But I don't feel like talking and I can't bear listening to the nonsense he spouts.

Once again he raises an arm and points to the bird. The waves roll into his lunatic grin, and just before he speaks I see the giant sea beast circling below, feel its undertow. It has returned. And this time Dad spots it too. He almost leaps out of the water.

"It's the Great Worm!" Dad shrieks. But then the sea covers his head and he's gone.

I flap about, trying to stay buoyant, stunned by the image of the beast below me. I've just seen Dad disappear and now I swallow a huge mouthful of sea water and feel myself slip under too. As I begin to drop down through the grey depths, all I can think about is how I'm going to die hungry. It just doesn't seem fair.

TWO

A dazzle of sunlight flashes through the water as I descend into a cloud of blue-green plankton. The weight of the cold sea pushes me down into inky-black darkness.

But a sudden current, surging from below like a giant hand, propels me back to the surface. I come up again, coughing and spluttering. I gulp the air and look for Dad.

I scream for him in a way I haven't for years.

"Daddy! Daddy!"

A few of our meagre possessions bob on the heavy swell: there's Dad's battered hat, the spotted handkerchief and a ping-pong ball. I pluck them out of the water, push the handkerchief and the ball into my pockets and pull the hat down tight on my head.

Dad is probably in the belly of the great creature. In a minute or two it will be my turn.

The people of the Fury Islands warned us of the Great Worm. As we paddled off in their tiny fishing boat they yelled at us from the shore, "Thieves! Beware the Worm! The Great Worm will revenge us for your crimes!" And now one of their superstitions is about to have me for breakfast.

I try to look down into the water but can see nothing but coils of weed.

And then with a sudden, thunderous heave of water the Great Worm comes up behind me.

I close my eyes and feel oddly peaceful. I see my mother's face, her kind, warm smile. In a few moments I will be with her. Dad will be there too and is probably already telling her how Mother Fortune showed him the way.

I'm almost laughing at this as a huge wave breaks over my head, then another, and I'm waiting for the big dark mouth. But it doesn't come.

I open my eyes and there it is, gliding past, a long, gleaming mustard-brown fish. I can almost reach out and touch it. It's a basking shark. There is no Great Worm.

It seems to go on and on, a colony of creatures living on it: barnacles and limpets, gleaming clinging things and stars of gooey life.

When it has pushed past, carving through the water, I hear Dad's voice. He's still alive!

"Look at these weeds, Oswald!" he yells, the words bouncing like a skimmed stone across the levelling water.

He's grinning and peering down into the sea, his hair plastered flat to his head, his eyes sparkling. I want to scream with joy. I want to thrash across the water and hug him. But I see that glazed look on his face and I know he has seen a sign.

"The weeds form a word!" He looks up again at me, squinting into the sun.

"The weeds spell 'WEST'!" He looks triumphant. "Oh, Mother Fortune. Thank you. Thank you again!" And he raises his arm like a military commander and hollers, "This way!"

I watch in horror as he launches into a long, lumbering stroke, his legs kicking behind him. He doesn't wait to see if I follow.

"And," he splutters back at me, "that hat is far too big for you, Oswald!" He begins laughing, then starts to choke on sea water.

"What are you doing?" I scream. "We can swim to safety if we go –" and I take a deep breath to scream even louder – "that way!" But he doesn't even look back.

I tread water for a few moments and watch him push ahead. I'm struggling to catch my breath but there's no choice. I begin to swim after him, smashing my hands on to the surface with a violent rage. I don't keep it a secret from myself: I'm imagining smashing his stupid face in.

I don't know how long I trail behind him. I know that I can't catch up. My thoughts drift to the City Museum. I am a toddler again, holding my mother's hand. We're looking up at the big fish hanging from the ceiling; it looks like it's flying through the air. It has its mouth wide open, wider than seems possible. It's a basking shark.

Mum used to take me to the museum all the time. I loved it, even though it gave me the creeps. All those long corridors, lit by a peculiar yellow light. And the eyes of all the dead creatures stare out at us from their glass cases. I'm staring back at them, wondering who will be the first to blink.

Mum would lean over my shoulder and whisper things like, "One day, Oswald, you will be a great scientist. You will help unravel the many secrets of the natural world." But when she died my hopes of being a scientist died too. Instead I became an unwilling apprentice to my father, a witless conjurer who changes his name every five minutes.

A voice calls out and, for a moment, I think it's Mum. I lift my head above the water long enough to look. The shout comes again, a woman's voice. This time Dad turns too.

A small boat is moving towards us.

"Ahoy!" Dad yells, a long arm reaching so far out of the water it seems almost impossible. "You see!" he chirps gleefully. "The weeds were right, we are saved! We are saved!"

Which means I get to spend another day on earth with Dad. I don't know if I can bear it. Perhaps it would have been better if the Great Worm had got us.

THREE

Arms reach down, one a woman's the other younger, a girl's.

I have no strength left to lift myself, but feel them grab hold of me and pull me up into their small boat.

"Lovely hat," says the woman.

I lie face down in the boat for a few minutes, letting the sea water dribble out of my nostrils. I feel the boat tip as Dad struggles in. I am exhausted but seething with rage. I don't want to be saved by seaweed. I know I should feel happy to be alive, I should be crying with joy but I'm not. My life is predicted by seabirds and seaweed – the magical signs of Mother Fortune.

"Welcome aboard," says the woman. "I don't normally go around giving lifts to strangers.

"Elizabeth Evans," she says. "And this is my daughter, Bella. Here, have our coats, you must be cold. What happened?"

I keep my face down in a puddle of sea water.

Whatever story Dad comes up with now, I don't want to hear.

"Jeremiah O'Connell," he says, giving himself yet another new name. It makes me squirm. "And this is my son."

I'm dazzled by daylight as Dad takes the hat off my head.

"Well, Jeremiah," says the woman, "you are lucky to be alive. And so are you. . ."

"Oswald," Dad says. At least he doesn't give me a new identity.

I push myself up and see faces staring down at me. Dad is grinning and winking. The woman has a weathered, handsome face, and thick golden hair that tumbles out of a wool cap. She stops rowing and looks suddenly confused. Her mouth hangs open. She stares at me, then switches her gaze to Dad.

It's as if she's just been told the world is about to end.

Then I see the girl, her heavy black boots, a summer dress and her sullen, suspicious face.

My eyes fall upon the small basket next to her, covered with a cloth. The end of a loaf of bread sticks out from one corner. I just stare into it, hoping to draw the bread nearer by the power of my will. The girl turns her head and looks away.

I look back at her mother. She still looks bewildered but has closed her mouth. She holds the oars level, as if waiting for a command to row. She blinks.

"Oswald O'Connell, did you say?"

Well, I am Oswald, but the surname is as new to me as it is to her.

"Bella?" she says, turning to her daughter, although her eyes remain fixed on me. "It's him. At last. I knew he was coming."

Her daughter scowls and the wind sweeps strands of her black hair across her face. She narrows her dark eyes. The woman turns to look at Dad, as if she wants to ask him something. But her daughter glares at her.

"Mum, please," says the girl. "They'll jump back in the water if you keep staring at them!"

Elizabeth Evans begins to row.

What does she mean, "I knew he was coming"? Who does she think I am? Dad is sitting there, smugly grinning, as if he knows something I don't.

"So where were you heading?" she says, her voice a little distracted.

"We were just touring," Dad says. "We are entertainers."

I notice Bella glance at us and then look back to the sea.

"Oh yes? And is that how you intend to pay your way?" Elizabeth's nervous laugh rings out over the water. "With singing and dancing? Just where do you plan to stay?" Her eyes flick over to me.

"I am a master conjurer," Dad replies, a little crossly. "We will have no trouble affording rooms in the most prestigious hotel."

Elizabeth runs her eyes over Dad, taking in his sodden, tattered clothing, his scrawny face and rough hands. I can see her make a swift calculation – this isn't a man who is used to luxury. She watches him theatrically search his pockets with a faint smile on her lips. I know what he is going to say next. I struggle up and wedge myself into the corner of the boat. Here it comes.

"I wonder, do you, by any chance, happen to have a hard-boiled egg or two? I could show you a rather wonderful feat of magic."

Elizabeth sighs. "I'm sorry, we haven't brought any with us. We're not big egg eaters, are we, Bella?"

Bella folds her arms and shakes her head. She doesn't seem to share her mother's amusement.

But we have a substitute: the ping-pong ball. I claw it out of my damp trousers and pass it to him.

The rhythm of Elizabeth's rowing immediately ceases. Bella watches, but looks somewhere between bored and suspicious.

Dad pushes the ball into his mouth, removes it from his ear, pushes it in his mouth, finds it in my hair.

"I usually perform this with a hard-boiled egg," he repeats, eyeing the basket.

This is where I have to sneeze. It's a distraction.

The ball vanishes. Dad looks from the girl to the woman, and then to me.

Elizabeth's eyes open wide in exaggerated admiration. The girl sits stiffly, unimpressed.

With a flourish Dad indicates the basket. "I believe you will find it in there," he says to her.

The oars are held up in suspense. Bella remains still for a few seconds, then, after an exchange of glances with her mother, removes the cloth that covers the food and reveals the ball.

Elizabeth gasps, keen to show her approval of Dad's magic.

Next Dad snatches something from the lining of his hat.

I look into the basket, where I can see the remains of a picnic: half a loaf, some cheese and a ham. My hunger is painful.

Dad's fingers start emitting smoke and

suddenly there's a flash. A feeble explosion of damp feathers momentarily obscures his face. Elizabeth laughs, then shakes her head and resumes rowing.

"Impressive," she says, without a trace of sarcasm in her voice. Then she looks at me. "Oswald O'Connell," she says, as if speaking my name out loud makes it less unlikely. "Do you know who you are, Oswald?"

"Mum!" Bella suddenly snaps. "Don't be ridiculous!"

"But it could be him, couldn't it? He could be the one, couldn't he? The letters spell it out clearly."

"What are you talking about?" I ask at last.

"You are the destiny of the island!" Elizabeth says. "You haven't come here by chance, you know!"

Dad sits up, suddenly alert. "Mother Fortune brought us here," he says. "She has saved us on many occasions."

Bella leans forward, deliberately trying to cut short this bizarre conversation. "Are you hungry, Oswald?" she asks.

I hear Dad speak for me: "Our provisions went down with the boat."

"Offer our passengers something, dear, we need

to look after them," says Elizabeth, now leaning powerfully into her stroke. "It shouldn't take too long before we get back to the island."

"What island?" Dad asks.

"Idlegreen," she replies.

I frown. I thought I knew every name of the line of rocky islands stretching out from the mainland: Faith's Test, All Sorrow, Many Winkles, Old Fang, Greater and Lesser Fury, Mardy End and the Craven Lighthouse. Then just open sea for a thousand miles. There isn't an island called Idlegreen.

"I can't say I know the name," Dad says, unperturbed.

"No," Elizabeth says. "It isn't a place known to the wider world. The Judge won't allow mapmakers anywhere near the island. He doesn't want to share too much of his good fortune."

"The Judge?" says Dad, trying to show interest.

"Judge Butterworth," Elizabeth replies, a sour look on her face. "Idlegreen is fortunate and blessed. But the Judge is a monster. Just hope you don't bump into him."

FOUR

Moments ago we were drowning, starving and about to be eaten alive. Now we are sharing a hamper of food and heading towards an island of plenty.

"Not far now," puffs Elizabeth.

I know I'm making the noise of a strangled pig and Dad is chomping noisily too, but the food tastes so good. He manages to pause for a moment to make conversation.

"So, may I ask, were you visiting friends? Have you come from the mainland, or one of the islands?"

"Oh no," Elizabeth answers, "we were not visiting friends. But we are returning from the mainland."

Dad doesn't know what to do now. I can see him looking at his food, hungrily eyeing the cheese. But he obviously feels the need to look less desperate. He tries to continue the conversation. "Then it must have been business," he says. Elizabeth shakes her head. Dad closes his eyes. "No? Then let me guess. Yes, I have it. You are an educator, a teacher, a professor of languages."

"No, Mr O'Connell," sighs Elizabeth. "A year ago a fishing boat was lost. My husband was one of the crew. It disappeared this time last year. There was a service, and we spent last night with the families of the fishermen."

There is an embarrassed silence. Dad fiddles with his cheese for a few seconds, then, when a respectable time has passed, he pops a chunk into his mouth. He chews slowly, staring into space.

The morning sun has turned the sea sapphire blue. Something swirls above. Butterflies, hundreds, even thousands of them, curving out over the waves, then turning back on themselves, following their own mysterious signs. They are purple emperors, black, speckled with white and flashed with indigo.

In the City Museum butterflies were pinned in neat rows, like military units. Mum would lead me along the cases and I would watch our reflections, like ghosts, moving across them. She would read the names of anything that caught her attention, or mine. The butterflies were so perfect and still.

I see a strange look cross Dad's face. I bite a piece of apple and try to follow his line of sight.

An island of green slopes and bright trees materializes from the morning haze.

Dad makes a sort of baffled "wuh" sound, which I suppose is a mixture of where and how coming out of a mouth full of bread.

"This is our home, Mr O'Connell," says Elizabeth. "Although not much of it is ours."

Dad loses all interest in his food. Ahead of us the lush green island rises out of the sea. Undulating pasture is dotted with sheep and cattle, and slopes of corn shimmer in the morning sun. There are vales of thick woodland and on a distant tor the broad blades of a white windmill rotate serenely.

The vision before us is an island paradise, overflowing with the bounties of nature.

Elizabeth heaves on the oars. She seems to be slightly amused at the expression on Dad's face. His jaw has dropped open, his eyes are two glassy buttons.

"How is this possible?" Dad mutters, "when everywhere else is so. . ."

"Good soil, sir, good soil," interrupts Elizabeth. "Especially for those that can afford it, like the esteemed and all-powerful Judge Butterworth. But perhaps his good fortune is about to end." She looks across at me again, this time with a fixed smile. I can tell she has something in mind. It gives me the creeps.

I would feel more comfortable if Idlegreen was another bleak rock, like Greater Fury, with rude inhabitants and feeble plant life clinging to its tired soil. This sudden abundance is eerie.

We approach the island, and are soon dwarfed beneath its sheer cliffs. I peer down into the water and can see the seabed, illuminated brilliantly by the sunlight. Every darting fish, scuttling crab, every shell and every rock is visible as if below glass.

I glance up at Elizabeth. She is still staring and smiling. "You will be coming with us, won't you?" she says.

Dad stifles a laugh. "Well, we don't intend jumping out of the boat, just yet, do we, son?"

"You really are Oswald O'Connell, aren't you?"

"Of course he is!" declares Dad.

Elizabeth nods towards Bella once more.

"It is him," she says. "The one the clocks speak of."

I lift myself up to see a small stone quay jutting out from the cliffs.

"We'll take the boat around the other side to moor it. Then we can show you Hook Head."

I can see Dad is a little taken aback by this. He

doesn't particularly want an escort. "Madam, you have been more than kind," he says, looking at Elizabeth with as much sincerity as he can muster. He stands suddenly and just about keeps his balance. "I hope I can return the favour one day." He grabs my arms, then leaps out of the boat, pulling me with him. We crash clumsily on to the weed-slippery edge of the quay. He gropes wildly for a few seconds, then hauls himself up. He drags me on to my feet.

"Wait," Elizabeth shouts, her voice suddenly urgent and alarmed. "Please, don't go!" One oar slips from her hand. She tries to stand but is unbalanced and can't gain a foothold. "Bella, it's him, I tell you. You heard his name!"

"Tricksters." Bella shrugs and refuses to move. "I can spot them a mile off."

We stand on the jetty for a few seconds, Dad checking around him. Elizabeth is still calling to us from the boat.

"Please wait," I hear her yell. "Please!"

"Right," he says, pulling down the soggy crumpled edges of his jacket. "Let's see what Hook Head has to offer."

Elizabeth makes one last plea. "You don't understand. Perhaps you don't realize who you are! Oswald, Idlegreen is your destiny!"

Dad nods towards the end of the quay and sets off for a long flight of stone steps cut into the cliff.

"What is she talking about?" I shout at him.

"The woman is obviously mad," Dad puffs, springing up the steps two at a time. "Now let's put a move on, we need to lose them."

At the top of the climb is a tall iron gate. It is locked. I push myself up to get a closer look at the hubbub of humanity that is Hook Head. Then the barrel of a musket is thrust through the bars and pointed straight into Dad's face.

fiVE

"Your business, sir?" croaks a flat, melancholy voice.

Dad straightens himself up. "My name is Jeremiah O'Connell. I am an entertainer, a conjurer. Your people enjoy such things, I imagine?" Dad squints between the bars and then checks the steps behind us.

"My business is not to imagine," replies the voice. "I am under instructions from Judge Butterworth to keep charlatans, thieves and beggars from disturbing things here. And you, sir, you look very much like all three."

Dad laughs at this. "Oh! This apparel?" he says, "I am afraid my son and I had an unfortunate mishap. Our vessel was sunk on our journey. Our rescuers set us down here but have travelled on."

"I don't need your life story, sir. And we don't need no more conjurers. We already have one. The Judge doesn't think he is very good but says he will do. And I wouldn't want to argue with the Judge."

I push closer to the gate to have a look at the gatekeeper. He is very round, with red cheeks and a bulbous, misshapen nose. His eyes are heavily bloodshot. He looks like he's just woken up, and as if he thinks we are responsible for waking him.

"My man," Dad says, leaning forward, and lowering his voice to a whisper. "I can also read fortunes. I can help you."

"Haven't heard that one today, sir," cackles the gatekeeper, his acrid breath causing Dad to flinch. The gun is removed from between the bars. "Five shillings will get you in, sir. Five shillings, and not your mumbo-jumbo."

"Five shillings?" shrieks Dad. "Five shillings? That's robbery!" Dad's voice has got that edge to it. He starts doing strange things when he gets like this.

"Well, it's normally sixpence. Sixpence to decent folk. But you look like a rogue. Five shillings, please."

Dad makes a scary croak, like a crow. He flaps his hands at his side, like little wings. We don't have five shillings.

Eventually Dad seems to bring himself under control. He looks up. "Do you see any clouds?"

"I see plenty of clouds," replies the gatekeeper. "But I see no shillings."

"Pick a cloud," says Dad.

"You pick a cloud, sir, and go back home on it," the gatekeeper cackles.

"Give me one chance to demonstrate my powers," begs Dad.

"Very well," the gatekeeper sighs and spits. "You want me to pick a cloud. Well. I've picked one."

"Now tell me, sir. Does the cloud remind you of anything?"

The gatekeeper continues to look up, a puzzled expression on his face. "Why yes, it does! Spit on my boots, sir, it does!"

"And what does the cloud remind you of?" Dad moves closer to the bars, encouraging the gatekeeper to concentrate. Dad has one arm behind his back. He is signalling something to me. It takes me a while, but at last, I get it. And he's getting restless again; he wants me to hurry. So I must take my chance. Dad wants me to push my hands through the bars and get at the gatekeeper's keys.

I don't look up but I hear the gatekeeper sniff. "It reminds me of a great teacher I once knew." I presume he hasn't spotted me, nor felt my fingers at his belt. "He looked like that, all crumpled in a heap."

Dad must keep him from looking down. The

keys are in my fingers, but I can't detach them. I can't do it.

"What, that cloud?" Dad presses close to the bars, urging the gatekeeper to keep looking up. "Why does that one remind you of your great teacher?"

"He looked like that after I shot him between the eyes for trying to fool me with his mumbo-jumbo!"

The musket appears between the bars once more.

"Judge Butterworth won't be very happy with me if I let the likes of you on to the island," continues the gatekeeper, agitated. "He'll have me shipped off to Gull Rock before I've had chance to open my mouth to explain." He pushes his face into the bars. "And that's where you'll end up if you sneak past me." He lowers his voice to a hiss. "And may God have mercy on your souls. Now clear off before I discharge this weapon in your direction."

I pull away from the gate. Dad bows and, after touching me on the shoulder, indicates we should go back down the steps. We don't seem to have a choice.

But coming up towards us are our rescuers.

"Mr O'Connell!" Elizabeth's voice reverberates

between the cliffs. "How kind of you to wait for us!" Her smile is one of relief and unconcealed joy. Bella is behind her, hauling up two baskets. "Your son, Mr O'Connell," she pants as she climbs, "I must speak with you urgently about your son."

"Why, of course, madam, it is the very least I can do."

Dad fixes a grin to his face and clasps his hands together like a kindly old vicar. I can't believe Elizabeth doesn't see straight through him.

"Let's get through the gate, then find somewhere to talk," she says.

"Good morning, Gerald," says Elizabeth.

The gatekeeper turns, a thin smile on his lips. But when he sees us, his face contorts. "Mrs Evans," he snarls, "are these friends of yours?"

"Oh, very much so," she answers.

He looks carefully from Dad to me. "Are you sure, madam?"

"Please open the gate, Gerald. We need to get home."

"Well, you'll have to be answerable to the Judge if they cause trouble, not me. You know what he's like."

"Yes, Gerald," says Elizabeth, "we all know what the Judge is capable of. Now please, let us in."

The gatekeeper leans up against the bars and,

without removing the keys from his belt, unlocks the gate.

As he closes it behind us, Elizabeth begins searching through a bag. "I'm sure I have some sixpences for you here, Gerald," she says.

The gatekeeper puffs his cheeks and scratches his head. Dad, meanwhile is looking for another opportunity to get away. This time he spots the gatekeeper's tiny wooden sentry box. He steps towards it and pokes in his nose.

Elizabeth, Bella and the gatekeeper are still huddled around the bags. "I'm sure I have one or two coins somewhere," Elizabeth is saying.

Dad pulls me to one side. "Look!" he whispers. I stand next to him and peer into the gatekeeper's booth. A plate of sixpences glitters invitingly on a shelf. I don't want Dad to touch them but there is no point in protesting. He scoops up a handful, a few spilling out and tinkling on to the floor. He looks at me in that exuberant way that I know will lead us into trouble. He empties the coins into his pocket, checks to see if the others are still distracted, then immediately pulls me by the sleeve towards the crowds on the streets of Hook Head. Dad almost bounces along, the coins jingling noisily and I run behind him, picking up the few sixpences that fall through tiny holes in his pockets.

"Mr O'Connell," shouts Elizabeth from behind us.

"Dad," I call out, "I think Elizabeth wants to. . ."

"Hurry up," he snarls, "I know. Come on. She's only after my money." Another sixpence slips out of the bottom of a pocket and rolls on to the street. I don't bother trying to pick this one up.

The pavement follows the cliff top, but on the other side of the road tall buildings with huge windows reflect the sun. I've seen streets like this in the city, but never so elegant and white.

I'm almost running now, trying to keep up with him. I dodge a line of well-groomed schoolchildren in a uniform of velvet and lace, a scowling schoolmaster behind them, urging them on.

"Mr O'Connell!" I hear Elizabeth yelling, her voice fainter now but still shrill and almost desperate.

We rush past a row of magnificent hotels, then circle a park in which huge trees surround a vast wrought-iron bandstand.

"I don't like the look of this place, boy," Dad says, "all this wealth. How can a place be so prosperous when everywhere else is so squalid?"

A huge store called Butterworth's opens on to the street. It displays pyramids of potatoes, mountains of green vegetables. Huge baskets of glossy-skinned apples and golden pears are everywhere, as if caught falling from the sky. Dad reaches out a hand and, without missing a step, snatches up two apples. The smell of baking drifts from an alley. A glossy white sign fixed to a wall states "Butterworth's Bakery" and beneath it a painted hand points left.

Dad continues to mutter away. "This Butterworth chap must have made a pact with the Devil, or else he has some other sinister secret. It isn't right, Oswald, just mark my words. It isn't right."

I pull at Dad's sleeve and nod towards one of the little pastry shops. He strides along the pavement, his head up, winking and grinning at every passer-by.

A horse-drawn carriage rattles slowly along the main street, moving cautiously and giving time for pedestrians to step aside. I move to the gutter, keeping my head down whenever anyone passes. We are clearly not islanders; we stand out a mile. Our damp clothes and grubby faces must mark us out as strangers.

There are shops overflowing with leather, with wicker, with candles and lamps, with ornate pots and glittering metalwork. Every shop is bursting with bright, new things.

"Gluttony, avarice," mutters Dad. "Pride goeth before destruction!"

There does seem to be more than enough of everything and there must be an explanation for it. But I wish Dad would stop his superstitious mutterings.

And suddenly there's a rumbling sound coming towards us. A man in a scarlet uniform and a little black cap guides a wheelbarrow of soil along the gutter. Behind him marches a second, in identical uniform and carrying a pike. "Get out of the way!" yells the first guard, stern and wary, as if his cargo is very precious. I jump up on to the pavement and he thunders past.

The second guard looks at Dad and then at me. I notice a small insignia on his cap, two silver "B"s, one reversed to face the other, eight silver lines radiating from it, forming what looks like a spider. On the back of his jacket is the same symbol and below it the words "Butterworth's Bank". Dad grabs my wrist and pulls me on. I turn to look back, to see if Elizabeth and Bella are behind us. There's no sign of them. Perhaps they have given up.

At the furthest end of the main thoroughfare we come to a cafe with seating outside overlooking the sea. Customers sipping hot drinks and eating pastries shrink in disgust as we move between them, a little slower now. Women in long, lace gloves glare at us from beneath parasols. Dad is still trying to maintain his dignity. He keeps his head up and stares above the astonished faces.

Dad points to the name over the cafe. "Well, who would have guessed it," he sneers, "look what it says, 'Butterworth's Restaurant'. Does the villain own the whole island?"

Once more a wheelbarrow of soil rumbles past, the scarlet-clad porter eyeing Dad suspiciously. The second guard, wielding a pike, passes close to Dad, who makes no attempt to step out of his way.

"Watch where you're going, Butterworth's barrow boys," Dad shouts. The guards are far from boys. They are old men, with silver hair and creased faces.

And then, above the conversation of cafe customers, I pick out a voice. "That's him, sergeant!" it says. "That's the thief!"

Six

There's a policeman walking briskly towards us. Beside him is a man whom I presume is a shopkeeper. I pull at Dad's jacket. I want him to run.

"If we run it's an admission of guilt," he hisses at me. Everyone is staring at us. Everyone. Dad stands to attention, his head held high and his back straight. The policeman, obviously expecting a chase, is a little taken aback.

"Excuse me, sir," says the policeman, "this gentleman believes you are responsible for the theft of apples from Butterworth's stores." The policeman says this with no hint of anger. He looks as if he has been disturbed from his tea and newspaper but blames the shopkeeper, rather than us.

"I really have no idea what you are talking about, officer," Dad replies.

"He has the apples in his hand, sergeant," says the shopkeeper.

"I can see that," says the policeman, a little annoyed.

"Officer, I do not deny these are apples," says Dad. "I did not steal them, however."

"Pardon me, sir," says the policeman, "but I know most people on this island. Who are you?"

I look up at Dad and wonder who he is going to be next.

"Jeremiah O'Connell," he replies. "My son, Oswald, and I are staying with my cousin, Mrs Elizabeth Evans."

The officer strokes his chin. He has a kind face, a little square moustache. His uniform is spotless, immaculate. "Mrs Evans? The owner of the shop at the Green?"

Dad nods, a little vacantly.

"Those are Judge Butterworth's best," puts in the greengrocer, "I'd recognize them anywhere. And more to the point, so would Judge Butterworth!"

"Indeed," says the sergeant, standing stiffly and adjusting the angle of his helmet, as if the Judge himself were present.

A small crowd has gathered around us now and is beginning to listen with interest.

Dad looks at the policeman and narrows his eyes. "My son and I were presented with these apples by Mrs Evans as we stepped off her boat on to the island. 'Welcome to Idlegreen,' she said. Some welcome this is!"

I nod. A small group of young men applaud.

"Well, you go and enjoy your apples, sir."

"I was intending to, officer. Good day," says Dad.

But as we turn away, and I can't believe Dad has got out of this so easily, I hear a voice I recognize and which makes my heart sink. "Hello again, my friend." It's the gatekeeper. He's waving his musket towards Dad's head. "Sergeant Smedley," he calls, "this pair saw fit to help themselves to my, er, tips."

The policeman waves a hand. "Point the gun down, Gerald, and we'll go from there." The gatekeeper does as he is asked. The policeman looks down at me and sighs. "Empty out your pockets, will you, boy?"

I look at Dad, and then the policeman. The sergeant's boots are so well polished I can make out my reflection, a tiny little creature stuck to the toecap. I turn my pockets inside out. There's nothing in them except a few crumbs of bread.

"And the old man's jacket pockets," snarls the gatekeeper, waggling the musket again.

This time the policeman doesn't make any

request. He simply takes hold of my father's jacket and shakes it. The jingling of sixpences fills the air. The policeman rolls his eyes; the crowd begins to laugh.

"OK, you two," he says quietly. "I'm afraid you're going to have to come with me." Dad holds out his hands and I do the same. The policeman produces a pair of shiny handcuffs, and after a little fumbling, manages to place one cuff around Dad's wrist, the other around his own. "Now, sir," says the policeman. "The station is just around the corner. I would be very grateful if you and your son would walk with me."

"Certainly, officer," says Dad. "Nothing would give me more pleasure."

Cheers and handclaps fill the air, sending seagulls flapping upwards. It's the best crowd we've had for a month, and certainly the best applause.

But a voice cuts the ovation short.

"Sergeant Smedley," it calls. "One moment, please." Elizabeth Evans steps out in front of us.

"Mrs Evans," says the sergeant. "How nice to see you. I'm afraid your cousin here is in a little bit of trouble."

Bella, standing beside her mother, raises her eyebrows.

"I know, sergeant," says Elizabeth, completely

unruffled by the surprise news that we are related. "I heard. I just wondered if young Oswald was also implicated."

Smedley turns to look at me, slightly bewildered, as if he has a new problem to solve. "Well, no," he says slowly, "I don't suppose he is."

"Because he is the one," says Elizabeth, taking a step forward and pointing at me. "He is the one on the clocks. You know what I mean, don't you, sergeant? He is the one we've been waiting for! We must take care of him!"

Someone behind me mimics Elizabeth, ridiculing her. "He is the one!" they squeak. "He is the one!" A wave of laughter rolls across the crowd. It's not just me that thinks she's talking nonsense.

"She's nuts, sergeant," someone else shouts. "Lock them all up!"

Smedley looks a little bewildered.

The crowd has grown and begins to jeer and whistle noisily. Some spectators have climbed on to the sea wall to get a better view; others stand on cafe seats. There is more laughter, then I'm shoved from behind and stumble forward. "Careful," someone calls, "the special one might get hurt!" The laughter is louder and becoming threatening and the look on the sergeant's face suggests he doesn't know what to do. A cream cake flies over his head, and then a bread roll. There are more taunts and the sound of fists thumping a tabletop.

And then, suddenly, everything goes quiet.

Two scarlet-uniformed guards appear from nowhere. One grips a pike in two hands. Like the other guards, they are not young men. They have stern, weathered faces. "Is there a problem here, sergeant?" says one.

"I have arrested this gentleman," says Smedley, nodding towards Dad. "The crowd is getting a little excited, that's all."

"So I gather," says the guard. He turns to look at Elizabeth and then at me. "And did I hear someone say this is the one that the clocks speak of?" He raises an eyebrow. "Well, I am sure the Judge will be interested to hear that."

Elizabeth's face tenses. She steps forward. "If there are no charges against him, sergeant, I think the boy should come home with us. That's all right with you, isn't it, Jeremiah?" Dad is baffled, speechless. "They were coming to stay with us, after all," she says, reaching out for my hand.

"I am sure the sergeant has no objection, Mrs Evans," says the guard. "Indeed, I am sure, after what you have told us, that Judge Butterworth will be keen to meet the young man."

I feel Elizabeth's hand close tightly over mine. I hear Bella snort and see her glare at her mother.

Sergeant Smedley, a little confused, goes to scratch his chin but has forgotten Dad's wrist is shackled to his. "Yes, fine," he says at last. "The boy can go with your cousin, Mr O'Connell. He'll be safe there until we can sort this out." He nods across to the old guards. "Thank you, Angus," he says. "And you, Roger."

Dad looks bemused, then, as Smedley leads him away through the crowd, a little alarmed. He peers back over his shoulder, squinting into the sunlight, frowning. Then he looks at me, his features suddenly drawn.

"Make sure you find out what they want," he barks at me. "You don't get something for nothing."

He raises his hand towards his face, the policeman's wrist to his, and takes an enormous bite out of one of Judge Butterworth's apples.

The sergeant pulls him away, then, just as they are about to disappear into the crowd, Dad calls back to me.

"Watch the skies for signs, Oswald," he spits, pieces of apple spraying over the policeman's shoulder. "Mother Fortune speaks to us through signs! Watch the skies!"

SEVEN

When we lived in the city, when Mum was still alive, Dad worked six days a week in a brush factory. On Saturdays Mum would take me out, to the park, or to the museum. On Sundays Dad would help me fix my bicycle, or he would ask me to give him a hand while he put up some shelves or repaired a leaking pipe. On weekdays I used to go to school. It was a nice, safe, ordinary life. I liked it. I won a place at the Institute to study science and Mum was so proud of me. I had everything to look forward to.

But then she died and Dad lost his job. Soon we began this desperate new life, travelling from town to town trying to make a few pennies from conjuring. It took a while but eventually I got used to the hunger and spending nights under hedges and in sheds. But when I fall asleep I still dream about things as they were. So much has gone.

Leaving Dad behind and heading off with strangers, it isn't as tough as it could be. In fact, it's a bit of a relief. Even if one of them does think I'm something I'm not.

The hard bench at the back of the trap is just about big enough for the three of us and, as it bumps through the streets of Hook Head, we're thrown sideways, swung this way and that; we thump shoulders and accidentally kick each other. A small, mean-looking man sits opposite us. He smokes a pipe and keeps picking his nose. He stares at me and now and again releases a cloud of white smoke. He has teeth like gravestones and skin like smoked fish.

We drive up into open farmland, the sky widening. The air around us changes, becoming colder and damper. To our right is the sea – it ploughs into the rocks below, jagged and wild on this west coast, so different from the smooth waters I saw at the quay at Hook Head.

"You don't know how important you are to us, Oswald," says Elizabeth, smiling.

The mean-looking man takes his pipe out of his mouth. "This little chap the answer to all your problems is he, Mrs Evans? I've heard you've told most of Hook Head. Judge Butterworth will be keen to meet him."

I've only been on the island for five minutes and I'm known to just about everyone.

Elizabeth leans towards me. "I'm sorry about all this," she says. "I'll try and explain soon."

Bella leans forward and looks directly at me, scrutinizing me. I stare back at her for a moment, then look away.

Ahead the road curves round, and we rise up to the top of a crest.

"Wolfgang," says Elizabeth, "can we stop here for a few seconds?" The pony slows and the trap comes to a halt. The little man opposite us frowns. "You can see all of Idlegreen from here, Oswald," she says, as if I should be interested.

Below us the island falls away.

I look back the way we have come, back to the parks, buildings and gardens of Hook Head. The island is a shallow bowl surrounded by several rocky tors. It looks like the ruins of a medieval castle, with high turrets of rock on each corner.

The little man opposite us pulls out his pipe. "I didn't realize this was a tour of the island!" he snaps. "Put a move on." Immediately the trap pulls away again. The pipe smoker grins unkindly. "I don't suppose business is any better, is it?" he asks Elizabeth, tapping on her knee with a haddocky hand. "Things still as desperate?"

"Business is fine, thank you," she replies, removing his hand.

"We still have a little matter to discuss," he says, releasing a snake of smoke that sweeps across the cab towards us. I notice Bella deliberately turn her face away.

"I would rather not discuss it now. Tomorrow, Mr Blight. I shall settle what I owe you tomorrow."

"Very well," he says, and seems satisfied with her answer. He sits back and folds his arms.

Elizabeth looks into the distance, obviously upset. She forces a smile and tries to educate me. "Most of the produce you saw at Hook Head comes from these tor farms," she says. Blight rolls his eyes. "And the farms that have an abundance of the old ash in their soil are the wealthiest of all," she sighs. "Unfortunately we don't have a great deal ourselves."

Turning a corner we meet a cart coming the other way. At the reins is one of the wheelbarrow porters I saw in Hook Head, dressed in the same scarlet jacket and wearing the small black cap. The horse he's guiding is leading an open wagon loaded with soil, and this is held in place with a fine scarlet net. A porter brandishing a pike stands on a step at the back. The cart squeezes past us. I notice Blight raises his hand to the guards; the first nods in acknowledgement, the second raises the pike in salute. Along its length the wagon has "Butterworth's Bank" painted in stark black capitals, and at either end of it is the spider insignia.

"And there goes a shipment of the very best ash," Elizabeth whispers, "on its way from Judge Butterworth's farm." She pauses for a moment then leans over and adds, "It's Butterworth who'll decide what happens to your father."

Butterworth. His name was everywhere in Hook Head. He owns the bank, the bakery and the huge greengrocer's. This is not a man to mess with. If the mean little farmer opposite us is right, then Judge Butterworth will be keen to know what I'm doing here. I wish I knew myself.

Still skirting the edge of the island, our trap descends a gentle path, and then comes to a standstill midway down one of the tors. This tor is a tall beacon, its summit is skeletal. Here the granite bones of the island are exposed. A thin, slightly twisted, stone building sits at the top. Smoke threads its way from the chimney in the uneven slate roof and weaves up into the low cloud. Yet the lower slopes of the tor could not be more of a contrast: they are lush with vegetation.

Blight climbs out of the trap. "I shall be calling

tomorrow, Mrs Evans," he says, still gripping his pipe in his teeth. Then, without another word, or even a glance in the direction of the driver, he turns and makes his way through a gate, up a narrow path towards his crooked house.

"Good riddance, Hugh Blight," hisses Elizabeth under her breath. "You wouldn't believe he was a wealthy man by looking at the condition of his ramshackle farmhouse, would you? He won't part with a penny unless he has to. Just hoards it."

We skirt Blight's farm on the seaward side, returning to the higher, coastal lane. A little further on I see a tor that seems, in comparison to Hugh Blight's, in robust good health. It is a vast sprawling belly of rock. Sitting just below the top is a splendid columned mansion, luminous and white.

"There," says Elizabeth, "is the tasteless pile of Judge Butterworth." A few smaller, neater houses and several barns and sheds surround it. I begin to make out orchards and plantations, a patchwork of colour and vigour. "Judge Butterworth doesn't own the island," says Elizabeth, "but he might as well. He has the best soil and the most land. He thinks he is the emperor of this place, Oswald. But he's a clown. And I have a feeling that, soon, now that you're here. . ."

But a look Bella gives her mother stops her in mid-sentence.

"I just hope he has time for your father," Elizabeth adds.

Below us a sea mist sweeps in between the tors and crawls down towards the basin of the island.

"And there," says Elizabeth, "is the Green. See the place near the crossroads? That's our home, the stores. And it's going to be your home, too, for a while."

I don't like the way she says this. And nor does Bella, by the look on her face.

A few houses are huddled up around the stores, and these few buildings sit beside a vast expanse of heath. There's no sign of life down there. The words "the Green" suggest a friendly little community with children flying kites, dogs chasing cats and nice old people taking the air. I'm a little disappointed. Although big, wealthy farms surround it, "the Green" is a bleak wasteland.

"Idlegreen has been waiting for you, Oswald," says Elizabeth. This makes my stomach turn over. "I sense a new era is about to dawn." She sounds like Dad.

Bella shakes her head and sighs.

The trap makes a sharp left turn and begins a

steep descent. The sun is ahead of us, just above a tor on the opposite side of the island. But it is obscured as we descend into cold, dark shadow. An unpleasant chill creeps over me. We seem to enter a realm of dense nothingness. We're in the crawling sea mist.

Wolfgang twists and shouts to us, "The haar, it's bad this morning. Much thicker than usual." The pony is pushing blindly down a strip of lane that rolls under us and is absorbed into the whiteness. "Never known the mist as bad as this," Wolfgang complains, obviously struggling to slow our descent.

The trap begins to shake, and then seems to be slipping from under us. The driver panics and begins yelling. The pony rears. Wolfgang is jolted up and is suddenly flipped out of his seat. The pony lurches to the right, the trap tips and continues, half on the lane and half in the ditch, its fragile wooden frame bouncing and jarring, crashing against boulders and spitting up clumps of soil. Elizabeth somehow sinks down, protected, but Bella is almost standing upright, countering the angle of the trap. I can't hold on and am flung out into the air.

I whirl up through silky, silvery light, then burst through the dense shroud of whiteness. I'm rising above the churning sea mist, arcing through the bright air like a leaping fish. At the summit of my climb I see something low in the sky, just above the horizon, a strange blurred star, a vague spiral. Then I plunge down, back into the mist, towards murky forms that become the trap, the pony, the lane, spinning below me, accelerating up and hitting me smack in the face.

EiGHT

I thought being swallowed whole by a sea monster would be a grim way to depart this life. But here I am, suffering a far worse fate. I am buried alive.

I lie awake in complete darkness. For a moment or two I consider that I might be dead already. This feels like a tomb. I can smell the earth that weighs down on me.

My face hurts. My head thumps. I'm not dead. I'm blind.

My shoulder aches. I begin to try and explore with my hands, but my arms are locked down. It's my burial shroud, bound tight.

No, just sheets wrapped tightly around me, that's all.

I lever myself up. I can still smell a thick stink of soil and something else, nearer, thick and musty. This, I soon discover, is the stench of heavy curtains, next to my face. I fumble and rummage with them and eventually daylight, like refreshing water, streams in.

I squint into the light and see a small back garden. A crumbling brick wall surrounds it and beyond this, a lane, then a scatter of cottages. Towering above these, some distance away, are two of the island's formidable tors. Low cloud hangs over the island, grey and heavy.

I pull back the curtains as far as they will go. Then I notice the guard; the scarlet of his jacket is unmistakable. He appears from behind one of the cottages, takes a few steps forward and stares directly up at me. I am being watched.

Turning away from his gaze I notice the source of the smell I thought was the earth above me. In one corner of the room is a stack of wooden crates crammed with potatoes. And hanging in the air, the shaft of sunlight illuminates a finer, grainier substance. Idlegreen ash.

I realize I must be in a room above the stores. But the place is silent, there's no sound to help me find my way out of here. I move across the room and reach for the door. I find myself on an upstairs landing of bare floorboards and peeling wallpaper. At one end there's another stack of potatoes. The whole place reeks of damp soil and I can taste the dusty particles of ash. A big window above the stairwell looks out over the island. The place looks grim, bleak and a little sinister.

Elizabeth called me the destiny of this place. I have no idea what she means, but it doesn't exactly feel like an honour.

I stop to listen for voices. Nothing. I creep down the stairs, back into darkness. A door leads to a neat, cosy kitchen, a range radiating heat, an old armchair in the far corner, a breakfast table, chairs and some eggs in a basket. This leads to a cooler, narrow storeroom with tall shelves running the length of it. The low shelves have a few boxes, one or two crates and bottles, lines of loose onions and earthy vegetables. The top shelves support some odd stubby clay urns. At the far end is a closed door.

I stand and listen for a while. I can hear something, a faint shuffling, something being moved about.

I nudge open the door, just enough to peer through the gap. There, in a big oak-beamed room that seems to take up both storeys of the house, is Bella, perched high on a heavy dark ladder, stacking shelves and rearranging things. I watch her as she pushes bags of sugar into line then marshals what look like jars of honey and dusty packets of tea. She cajoles washing-up powder and soap into an orderly line. Then suddenly she gives a loud cry, a sort of bark. I think for a minute she's seen me. But she hasn't. She's yelling at a packet of biscuits that won't stay upright.

The shop looks too neat, too orderly. It doesn't look like it has many customers. It's more like a museum than a shop.

Bella turns, and with a look of severe concentration on her face, suddenly sees me. I don't try to hide. I push open the door wide, so it doesn't look like I'm spying. "Oh," is all she can manage.

She descends the ladder, then lifts the thick, hinged section of a counter that separates me from the floor of the shop. She stands there for a moment, holding the dark wooden rectangle almost vertical with the palm of her hand.

"Nightmares over now?" she says. "Finished your yelling, special one?"

I don't know what she's talking about. I want to tell her about the guard in the lane, but now doesn't seem like a good idea.

She brings her face close to mine. Her eyes are narrowed with rage. "My mother thinks you're her saviour! I think you're a fraud. But, if you are going to stay here until Judge Butterworth can decide what to do with your father, then you're going to work hard." She pauses and her face hardens. "Your job, Oswald, is to keep an eye on things." She fixes me with her stare. "Mum thinks you will bring us good fortune, she even thinks you'll be useful. I don't. I think you'll just get in the way."

Great. Think of what we'll get done here. Me, keeping an eye on things while she moves them about a bit.

She brushes past me into the storeroom, closing the door behind her.

I step out from behind the counter on to the flagstone floor of the shop. I want to see what's on the shelves. I read each label carefully. I have no idea what most of them are.

Runyan's Pilchards in oil
Pascoe's Soap
Chambers' Jellied Pork
Pumpillion's Salve
Sloogwood's Finest Sauce
Pascal's Tincture

On the highest shelves are old bottles. They look like poisons and medicines, arranged in groups according to colour: there are brilliant deep blues and syrupy browns. Some are corked; others have screw tops. I can't believe anyone ever buys any of them.

"The ledger," says Bella suddenly. She is standing in the doorway to the storeroom. She holds out a large leather-bound book and then drops it with a thump on the counter. "Mum assumes you can write." I don't rush. I stand at the counter and turn the ledger so it faces me. "Open it," she orders.

I slide in my thumb, open a random page and flatten it out. There are lists of names and figures. The writing is a blotchy scrawl.

by Miss Hobbes, of Fortune Row, one loaf of bread ~1s 3d
by Mrs Drinkwater of The Aspens, a bottle of Weston's Stout ~2s 4d

"You must stay *behind* the counter when you're serving a customer," she says, pointing just in case I can't work that out for myself.

I twist myself through the opening, rotating the ledger with my hands as I do so. Bella marches in the opposite direction, and, raising her arm behind her as she passes it, flicks down the open slab of counter. It falls like an executioner's axe, making my heart race and sending a low vibration up through the beams and into the walls. Bella hauls another pile of something up a ladder. She glances down at me and breathes out noisily. She shakes her head and begins rearranging things.

I study the ledger.

Then the shop door crashes open. It's Hugh Blight. He glares at Bella and grabs a box of matches from the counter, scratching away at it until a flame crackles to life and smoke drifts through the shop. Bella turns her head away.

"Where's your mother?" he growls.

"Out, Mr Hugh, sir. Gone out," she answers him, not meeting his eye.

"Gone to Hook Head, has she? Gone to try and borrow some money to keep this place afloat?" Blight's face is thin and craggy, like his tor.

"No, Mr Hugh, she's out walking, that's all."

"Is that what she does when her business is collapsing around her? Goes for a walk?" Hugh Blight spits on the floor. "She said I'd be paid today. Said I'd be paid before anyone else."

"Sorry, Mr Hugh, sir, sorry," answers Bella, a tremor in her voice. She's pushing some bags of flour around but she's not thinking about what she's doing.

"Well, I'm not going home empty-handed." He throws open the counter and barges through into the storeroom. Bella almost falls down the ladder.

"No, no, you can't take any. No!" Bella goes to follow him into the storeroom but he's back in seconds. He stands in front of the door, holding one of the squat clay pots between two gnarled hands.

"I told her I would take one if I wasn't paid. She should have listened."

Bella stands in the centre of the shop, her face white.

Then he sees me.

"Hello again, young sir." A thin, unpleasant smile slides across his mouth. His pipe is gripped in his teeth and is furling out smoke. "These people are the scum of the earth," he snarls. He moves to go. Clutching the jar to his chest with one hand, he wrenches at the door. Just before he steps out he turns to look at me. "They can't go on for much longer, you know. They owe everyone money." He looks across at Bella. "This is a sinking ship," he says, leaving the door open and the shop full of his smoke.

NINE

There are two guards now, watching from either side of the stores. Bella has noticed them too.

"Ash wardens," she says. "Butterworth is making sure his men keep their eyes on you." She sweeps the floor. "That's what happens if you're the one on the clocks." I don't miss the sarcasm. She stops sweeping for a moment and holds the brush like the warden gripping a pike. She looks dangerous. "And you don't have to yell out in the night to pretend you're the chosen one!" I don't know what she's talking about. "Mother Fortune will signal the fate of Idlegreen!" she bellows. "And that's not all," Bella continues. "Watch the skies for signs! A new star! A new star!" She hollers this with her eyes closed, obviously imitating me. Some of the bottles rattle on the shelves. "Keeping us all awake with your rubbish!" She returns to the sweeping, thumping the brush into the walls with an undisguised fury.

One of the ash wardens is passing in front of

the stores. He peers into the window, looks at me and saunters off. Then he turns to look across the Green. He has seen something.

I press my face up against the window. Bella stops brushing.

I can hear a bird singing, and, far away, from the direction of Judge Butterworth's tor, the sound of hooves. There's a carriage drawn by two horses. Not ponies, these are proper, big glossy horses. The driver is elevated at the front and two figures lounge comfortably in the large open coach that follows.

The closer it gets the more lavish it appears. The carriage has a rain hood, but this is folded back behind the passengers. The body of the vehicle is polished black wood, which now and then reflects the bland grey sky. It circles the Green and heads towards the stores.

Bella has heard the hooves and stares through the panes of glass in the door. "Oh no," she says. "Not them."

I watch as the carriage pulls up. The warden steps forward to greet it, opening a door. Two tall well-dressed men, with close-cropped hair and heavy brows step down from the carriage. They listen to something the warden tells them, then look up at the stores. They spot me in the window and approach the door.

"The Butterworth boys," says Bella. "The Judge's twins. I think they've come to have a chat with you." She lifts the counter and ushers me out.

The door opens slowly and the two men step inside. Their movements are slow and deliberate.

"Oswald O'Connell?" says one.

I nod.

"Father would like to talk to you," says the other.

They move apart as if inviting me to step between them. I don't have much choice.

I sit between them in the carriage, and it pulls away. As the carriage turns in front of the stores I see the warden standing beside them. The second has joined him. They look like sentries. Bella is in the doorway. She has a hand over her mouth.

The carriage moves quickly but the ride is smooth. The twins sit stiffly beside me and say nothing. My stomach clenches and I can't work out whether it's hunger or fear. I think it's both.

We thunder towards Butterworth's mansion. It sits on the side of a huge tor, overlooking the Green, and is surrounded by magnificent trees and a thriving estate. The scarlet jackets of ash wardens are everywhere; some seem to be directing work below the fruit trees, others are moving in and out of a stone barn. A small group loads a cart.

The horses slow and we roll through the gates and up a long avenue, a drive that rises towards the house at the top. It is a huge place, bright and impressive against the grey, overcast sky. The drive splits before the house; we take the route that leads along the side that overlooks the cold, craggy sea.

We come to a stop in a cul-de-sac. One of the twins taps me on the shoulder and together we climb down from the carriage. It pulls away almost immediately, leaving us at the foot of narrow steps. One twin leads the way, the other walks behind me. I am not going to be allowed the chance to slip away.

We emerge on a wide terrace overlooking a grand lawn. A gardener is mowing. Another kneels and attends to flowers. Handsome trees stand at the far end of the gardens, rising up towards the summit of the tor. I am shown to a seat at a large, round, wrought-iron table. There is a tray on which stands a jug and some glasses. One of the brothers places a glass in front of me and pours from the jug.

"Is the boy here yet?" a voice booms from inside the house. He emerges from the depths of a large plant-filled conservatory that leads on to the terrace. It's the Judge.

His eyes meet mine immediately. With two flicks of a hand he indicates to his sons their presence is no longer required. He stands and regards me as a biologist might inspect a grub. He is the most ridiculous human being I have ever seen.

He wears a bright pink frock coat that bulges over his huge bulk. His legs, in pale-blue breeches, appear comically small in proportion to the rest of him. His shoes have ornamental buckles fashioned into the insignia I have come to know already, the Butterworth spider. This costume would be ludicrous in itself, but this isn't enough for the Judge. His face is daubed in powder, his lips are painted and pouting, and on his head is a colossal silver wig.

He looks like a decorated potato.

"Please taste the apple juice," he bellows, loud enough even for the gardener mowing the lawn to hear. "I am eager to know what you think of it."

I do as I'm told. The juice is very good. I nod.

The Judge pulls out a chair and sits down opposite me. He folds his arms across his wide chest and stares down his nose at me.

"I have been told by one of my wardens that

you are the one on the clock. That you are the one who has come to reverse the fortunes of the humble and meek of the island." His head falls back and he howls with laughter. With a flourish he pulls a lace handkerchief from a pocket to dab his eyes. "I'm so sorry," he shouts. "But how could you, a grubby little urchin . . . I mean. . ." And this sets him off again. His shoulders shake and a faint cloud of powder rises from his wig.

Then suddenly his expression changes. Without warning he jumps from his seat, his paunch shoving the table violently. The glasses on the tray crash against each other and mine falls into my lap, soaking me with juice before tumbling to the floor and shattering.

He thrusts a finger towards me.

"You don't expect me to believe your name is really Oswald O'Connell, do you? You can fool them but you won't fool me."

He moves around the table until he is standing over me. "Listen, boy, I don't care who you are. This island is as good as all mine. Your father is a thief and a conman. He dared to pinch two of my apples! He stole from the Judge!" He clenches his fist and crashes it down on to the table. "I don't know what your silly game is, pretending to be someone you're not, but if you try anything,

anything at all to upset things here, then your father will remain locked up in Hook Head jail until he rots." Then his voice drops to a whisper. "Or perhaps I'll find somewhere a little less pleasant for the pair of you. Gull Rock hasn't been occupied for a while."

And with that he turns and disappears back into the house.

TEN

"So you've met the Judge, then, have you, Oswald?" Elizabeth ladles some vegetable stew out for me and sets it down before me.

"Made him walk all the way back," says Bella.

We're sitting at the table in the kitchen, Bella one end, me the other. It's early evening.

"What did the Judge want to know?" Elizabeth asks.

Bella is staring at me. "He doesn't speak much when he's awake," she says.

Elizabeth scowls at her. "There's no need to be so unpleasant, Bella."

I look into my stew. What if I say the wrong thing, what if the ash wardens are listening at the door? It's not worth the risk. I keep silent.

"I don't think you've really recovered from the accident yet," says Elizabeth. "The Judge should have been a little bit more sympathetic."

Bella snorts.

"Do you remember falling out of the trap, Oswald?"

I nod.

"You had an awful bump on the head. The rest of us were all right, even Wolfgang. He is so sorry. Says it was the mist, he's never seen anything like it." Elizabeth passes Bella some stew, then brings her own bowl to the table and sits down. "We managed to get the trap upright, took you back on it." She prods her stew with a spoon and looks up at me to see if I remember. "We got you back here, put you to bed. You slept quietly for several hours, then in the middle of the night you started talking in your sleep."

"Yelling," Bella says. "Chanting."

Elizabeth ignores her this time.

"The accident was yesterday morning, Oswald. You know that, don't you? You were unconscious quite some time."

I look into the hollow of my spoon. A tiny, upside-down face stares back.

"I told him what he was shrieking," Bella snaps.

Elizabeth reaches for a plate of bread in the centre of the table and offers it to me. I take a slice and smile.

Suddenly Bella erupts. She throws her hands in the air. "Watch the skies!" she shouts, mimicking me once more.

"Bella!" exclaims Elizabeth, dropping her spoon and holding up both hands. "Stop it!"

I must look pale, I certainly feel sick. Elizabeth leaps up and gets me a glass of water.

"Bella doesn't mean to be horrible," she says. "She's worried. And scared."

"I'm not scared!" Bella cries. "We've got ash wardens watching the house, Butterworth's boys marching in here. Anyway, who cares about the destiny of Idlegreen? We're already finished. Customers are helping themselves."

Elizabeth sighs, then looks across at me. "You saw Hugh Blight this morning?" she asks. "We owe him money. We owe all the tor farmers money. Some are quite good about it, they understand. Judge Butterworth says nothing, but I know what he's doing. He's waiting until we owe him so much he can just take the whole lot off us, the stores, our home, the Green."

"Blight just pushed past me into the storeroom and helped himself to a pot of the ash," says Bella. "Helped himself."

Elizabeth suddenly slumps into a seat. "I think this is all my fault," she says. "Things are not good here. And there's an old story that one day someone will come to reverse the fortunes of people like us. It's just a story, and I suppose I want to convince myself it's true."

"You've convinced the Judge too," says Bella. "Why else is he so interested in our friend here?"

After the meal is cleared away Elizabeth says we should go for a walk. We go through the storeroom, past the pots, out of the shop door and step into the lane. The stores are on a crossroads, and opposite is the Green.

We cross over and I follow Elizabeth through a gap in a stone wall. The road, the stone, the overcast sky are all the same colour, a dreary grey. Just along the lane an ash warden leans against the corner of a cottage. Elizabeth and Bella ignore him.

"The Green," says Elizabeth, "is land that's belonged to my family for generations. Funny isn't it," she adds, "I own almost as much land as Judge Butterworth, but it's worth nothing. Maybe if Butterworth gets his hands on it he will use his stores of ash to make it fertile." Elizabeth sighs. "We might as well own a desert."

I can hear Bella snorting behind us.

The Green seems to fill the lowest point of the island. It's a vast, desolate heath. Where the land begins to rise there are crops, and higher, on the slopes of the tors, orchards and lines of fruit bushes, lush and laden.

"But this soil here is paper thin," says Elizabeth. "We can't grow a thing."

The grass is sparse and clings on for its life. Even my footsteps seem to disturb the soil enough to scatter roots.

"It's the same in our yard," says Bella.

"But we still have some pots of the old ash," continues Elizabeth. "A few. And we can use it to grow vegetables, potatoes mainly." The potatoes stacked up in my bedroom. I can still feel the particles of ash on my clothes. "Ash is the currency of this place," says Elizabeth.

The wheelbarrows at Hook Head, and the cart we passed. The army of ash wardens that guards the stuff wherever it goes.

"Look what ash can do," says Elizabeth.

And with a wide sweep of her arm I understand completely.

"That's Hugh's place," says Elizabeth. "Blight Tor. Look what he's got up there. He's Butterworth's little weasel."

Blight Tor may be one of the smaller rocks, but its lower slopes are thick with wheat and, further up, fruit trees and sunflowers. The overcast sky is brighter to the west; it silhouettes the crooked house on the summit.

"Blight won't starve," says Elizabeth.

"I wish he would," mutters Bella.

"But the Judge has most of the money and the power," says Elizabeth. "Butterworth is the real big shot around here. He owns most of the ash as well as half the shops in Hook Head."

"And he's waiting for our little business to crumble, so he can make it his too," says Bella.

What I don't understand is why such a man seemed to get so upset about me. How can I be a threat to him?

Bella puts her hand on her mother's shoulder. "Tell him about the Clackers, Mum."

"Squeezed in there between Blight and Butterworth are the Clackers." Elizabeth directs my eye to a smaller, flatter tor. "Mrs Clacker keeps a dairy farm, but I don't know how she manages it. She has a useless son. Does nothing."

"Except stare," adds Bella.

"They watch us, Oswald. And they watch each other. Butterworth has a telescope on his balcony, and most of the tor farmers have binoculars." Elizabeth points up to Blight Tor. "If you look at the top of Blight's place, you'll see he has a decrepit pair of field glasses poking out of the roof." I see something reflecting a bead of sunlight in the centre of the slates, but can't make out exactly what it is. "And now of course,

Butterworth has given orders for his ash wardens to keep an eye on you." Elizabeth sighs. "I'm sorry, Oswald, it's my fault. I shouldn't have made such a scene in Hook Head. It's made things very difficult for you, hasn't it?"

That's putting it lightly. I get the feeling if I do so much as open my mouth he'll lock Dad up for good.

We turn and head back towards the stores. Behind it two tors, rounder and smaller than Blight's, are darker and seemingly less fertile. One has a windmill at its summit, white against the low cloud. I remember seeing it from their boat.

"You'll meet the tor farmers, one by one, I'm sure," says Elizabeth. I walk behind her, trying to take everything in.

"And there, look, Oswald." Bella points across the island, beyond the tor with the windmill. Through a shallow vale I can make out a grey wart below the horizon, jutting brutishly from the sea. "Gull Rock," Bella tells me. "Where it's said the Judge abandons his enemies."

With that happy thought in mind I follow mother and daughter as they slip back through the stone wall and cross the lane towards the stores. But then I hear a whistle, a merry little whistle and an odd whirring.

Just then, from around the back of the stores, a bicycle appears, upon it a slightly dishevelled postman.

"Hey! Bella!" he cries. "Mrs Evans, how are things?"

Bella suddenly looks coy, and deliberately assumes a pigeon-toed pose. She's shameless. The postman is not much older than me.

"Hello, Dusty," says Elizabeth. "Haven't seen you for a while."

"Been working up at Butterworth's. Pays more than this. But I couldn't stick it. His sons are awful." He drags a canvas bag around from behind him and digs inside. "Here you go." He hands Elizabeth a wad of envelopes. "Oswald!" he announces, as if I needed reminding. "Oswald O'Connell! There's a letter for you in there, boy!" He calls me boy on purpose. He calls me boy because that suggests he is a man. He isn't a man; he's a moron.

Two ash wardens stand together on the lane, still watching over us.

Elizabeth pulls my letter out of the bundle. My name, and the address of the stores, has been typewritten, but there are a few mistakes. The word "Stores" is spelt "Stoors" – it's been crossed out with lots of "X"s and written again. The envelope is pale blue and has IDLEGREEN POLICE HQ HOOK HEAD in tiny dark-blue capitals across the top.

It's from Dad.

ELEVEN

I don't open the letter until later. I've tried to keep Dad out of my mind as much as possible. There's nothing I can do for him, except make things worse. Judge Butterworth made it quite clear what would happen if I tried anything.

I'm sitting on my bed, with the curtains open; there's still enough light left in the evening sky to read. I hold the envelope in both hands, and, just as I'm about to open it, I have a sudden dread. What lunatic visions has he had now? I slide my finger under the gummed flap and tear upwards.

Dad's writing is like him, tall, thin and jerky. He crams in a lot on each page, so one line of writing gets knotted with the line above, or the line below. So here goes.

dear Oswald,
Im all right dont worry about me. Sergent
Smedley is looking after me I think Im getting

fat here he feeds me five times a day and he
doesnt shut the cell door any more and I can
wander in and out and use the tiperiter in the
office I did the envelope its good isnt it I wood
have ritten the whole letter with the tiperiter
but Smedley was looking over my sholder
trying to be help full saying things like you
press this to do that and so on and it was
difficult because I have to say some very
important things

what was Mrs Evans going on about when
she called you destiny have you found out yet

this place gives me the spooks something is
not right about it there is to much of everything
it cannot last

Mrs Evans thinks you have come to save
them from something what is it

I think you must get away from there I wish
I had stopped you going I think there is danger

last night I dreamed of a terrible catastrofe
mother fortune is trying to tell me something
watch the skies for signs
love from DAD

I have to read the letter three times before I can
put it back in the envelope.

I can still see his face, the last time I saw him,

contorted and crazy. "Watch the skies!" he yelled at me. No wonder I was shouting it in my sleep.

There is only one thing I've gained since leaving the city. I've been able to see the stars. When we lived in the city I would take my star map on to the roof of our block. Even on clear nights the lights of the city made it difficult to see much of the night sky.

But when we started travelling across open country the whole dome of the heavens opened up. I began to recognize all the constellations I had seen in books. I began to pick out the planets and the brightest stars.

But during those few seconds when I was thrown out of Wolfgang's cart I saw something above the horizon. It was a new star. "Watch the skies," Dad says. And now I have seen something I don't understand. I have seen a sign.

I push the letter under my pillow, and lay down my head. I want to go to sleep but I can't.

And then I hear an odd noise, like tiny fingertips drumming. It's coming from the window. Peacock butterflies are fluttering against the glass, bouncing and tumbling as if they want to get in. There aren't many of them, and now and again one lands and crawls up the window. The ghostly images on their wings are like the big, curious eyes of infants.

Mum told me that before I was born Dad used to be an actor. He couldn't read well, so she would help him learn his lines. When she saw him on stage, she told me, he was hypnotic. But he found it hard to leave the characters on stage, and sometimes came home thinking he was a king, a magician or a great explorer. He was offered bigger and better roles, but found it difficult to remember everything he had to say. Eventually, he gave up and found a job in the brush factory.

I would be sitting quietly reading books about science, about stars and planets, or about how the world looked millions of years ago, and he would stride past me, glance down and say, "Books, eh?" and disappear into another room.

Mum taught me how to read; but I can't remember reading Dad's writing before. He doesn't even use full stops properly, not that it bothers me. What really upsets me is the way he rambles like a madman. If someone were to get hold of one of his letters, if that nasty little Dusty opened one, I don't think Dad would ever be allowed out of prison.

And I'm trying to get to sleep when some of what Dad says runs around in my head. Since we got to the Green Elizabeth hasn't said much about my "destiny" or whatever it was. Is that because she has me here? I'm trapped here and she knows I have nowhere else to go?

I must have fallen asleep at last because the next thing I know I'm woken with a jolt.

Elizabeth is standing over me. She has a lamp and a glass of water. She's whispering something. "Hey, quieten down, you'll wake the tor farmers!"

At first I don't know what's going on. It's the middle of the night. I sit up slowly, and sip the water.

"You've been shouting in your sleep again."

Then I see Bella standing in the doorway.

"Only says anything when he's asleep. Interesting that, isn't it?"

I take another sip of water.

Elizabeth sits on my bed. I lie down again. "You seem frightened, Oswald. You were yelling something about a new star. You were yelling 'catastrophe'! Is there something you'd like to tell us?" She strokes my head, and I don't like that at all. It reminds me of something Mum would have done. I'd rather Elizabeth just told me to shut up and go back to sleep. I don't need sympathy.

"Look, Mum," says Bella, "we'll just feed him

and give him somewhere to sleep, and he can keep his selfish mad ramblings to himself. I'm going back to bed."

"Don't take any notice of her, Oswald," says Elizabeth. "You're frightening her, that's all. She's a good girl, she'll be all right when you get to know her." She keeps her hand on my head and stares down at me, smiling.

I turn over and her hand slips off. I hear her sigh. I get a sense of dread when I hear what she says next.

"I think you do know something, don't you, something you should tell us? Are you the one we've been waiting for? Are you really the one the clocks speak of?"

TWELVE

"You have had an extra hour in bed. You have had plenty of time to eat your breakfast. Now, I need help. Come on. We have a customer!" She yells at me because we have a customer. What will she do if she sells something? Set off fireworks?

I hear her stamping through the storeroom. I know she's there, standing in the doorway, arms rigid at her side. She has already called me twice, so I don't push my luck. I don't look up at her, but take my breakfast things and put them into the big white sink, and as slowly as I dare, saunter through to the shop.

A large man with a mop of curly white hair is standing looking up at Bella, who is searching for something on one of the highest shelves. The man is chuckling to himself and rolling a large jar from hand to hand. He has a big, cheerful face.

"Sorry, Mr Broadfoot, I can't find any."

"No matter," he says, still chuckling. "Not urgent."

I tiptoe to my position behind the counter. Broadfoot puts his jar before me.

"Good morning, Oswald," he says. He holds out his hand for me to shake. He already knows my name. "Frank Broadfoot, I keep the mill."

I shake his hand.

"I see the Judge has one of his wardens keeping an eye on things here," he says. "The man is frightened of you, Oswald. Do you have any idea why?"

I shake my head.

Bella stands three packets of biscuits and several bottles of beer on the counter. "Will that be all, Mr Broadfoot?" she says, staring at me.

I open the ledger. Next to it is a nibbed pen and big bottle of ink. I unscrew the top of the ink, dip in the pen. I write:

by Mr F. Broadfoot, of the mill,
3 packets of Empson's biscuits
6 bottles of Plumpton's ale

"You have a very fine hand," he says. "An extremely fine hand."

Bella cranes round to look. She stares at the ledger, then at me. She looks even more hostile. What have I done now? "Biscuits are sevenpence, ale is one shilling and tuppence," she snaps.

I have a bit of trouble with numbers.

"Eight shillings and ninepence altogether," Bella says quickly, before I've even begun to get the figures into my head.

"And the jam!" adds Broadfoot, placing the jar he had been rotating in his big hands next to the biscuits. I examine the label and, taking the pen, add:

1 jar of Westwood's blackberry jam 8d

"Nine shillings and fivepence, please," calls out Bella, halfway up the ladder.

Broadfoot laughs; his tummy shakes against the counter. "Well, we seem to have a good team here," he says, passing me a ten-shilling note.

The till is a curious beast, a huge ornate monster that sits on the far end of the counter next to the window. I stare at it, trying to work out what I'm supposed to do.

Frank Broadfoot can see I'm having difficulty and leans over, indicating, silently, which buttons to press, and in which order. "Sevenpence change, please," he whispers, and winks as I pass him the coins. "Thank you, Oswald," he says in a deliberately loud voice, "first-class service. I will come again." He places his goods into a basket he's brought with him. "So, you think you'll have some camphor in next week?" he says, turning towards the door.

"Hope so," says Bella. "Thank you, Mr Broadfoot!"

Broadfoot swings open the door and, with a nod and a smile, closes it behind him.

"You have a very fine hand," Bella repeats Broadfoot's words in a deliberately squeaky voice.

I try to see what it is she is doing now and she catches me looking at her.

"Sweep the floor," she says suddenly. "Brush is in the storeroom."

I wait a few seconds, then do as I am asked.

That morning there are just two further customers. One of the Morden family, a young man with long, greasy hair and more shabbily dressed than anyone I have ever seen, shuffles in, buys some rat poison and shuffles out.

by Richard Morden, of Morden Tor, one bottle of GP Rat Poison 9d

And then later:

by Terry Finch, labourer resident at Butterworth Tor, one packet of pipe cleaners, 2d

Both of them know my name. Both of them seem to know why an ash warden is stationed outside the stores.

I try to keep busy but there's next to nothing to do. When Bella announces it is lunchtime she locks the door and gestures for me to follow her into the kitchen. We have an egg sandwich and some pears. We eat in silence.

And then she says, "Mum and I look after the clocks on the Green. This afternoon I will show you how to wind them and look after them. When you see them you will understand why Mum thinks you are something special."

"The one the clocks speak of?" I say.

Bella stares at me. "Yes," she scowls. "But you don't fool me for a minute."

THIRTEEN

"There are ten clocks in and around the Green," Bella explains, "the clocks are ancient and must be wound every afternoon. Without fail. We are paid to maintain them. They must be dusted, oiled and wound. They occasionally break down, then they are taken to be repaired at Hook Head."

It's like being barked at by an annoying dog. She gets up, takes her plate and glass, washes them and places them on the draining board.

"Mum and I are paid from an estate, a will. If we miss a clock, we could lose a year's money. It's that serious. Today I'll show you what to do, so pay attention. After that you're on your own."

She disappears for a few moments and returns wearing a thick pullover and a sheepskin jacket and what looks like a small leather case under her arm.

She notices the look I am giving her. She sighs heavily, her shoulders slumping. "Right, ready?"

I follow her out. As we pass the counter she grabs some keys from the board on the wall. I suppose I must try to remember which ones she's taken.

"They are all labelled."

We make our way around the outside of the stores, following a narrow path that cuts through the garden I can see from my bedroom. We pass through a gate and along a track that crosses a wheat field towards a row of cottages on the lower slopes of Mill Tor.

And suddenly, behind us, there are two ash wardens.

When Bella sees them she stops and turns to face them. They come to a halt and stand there. One, with a long white beard, folds his arms. The other, whose piercing blue eyes are magnified by the lenses of his spectacles, is scribbling into a notebook he holds almost at the tip of his nose.

"Look," says Bella, her voice shaking as she tries to control her anger, "we're just going to wind the clocks. We're not planning a revolution."

The very old one, he looks almost ninety, nods his head. The spectacled one peers up at us.

"Why don't you just leave us alone? What have we done?"

The older one folds his arms. "You've done nothing, girl," he says. "Not yet, anyhow. But our orders are to keep our eyes on the boy."

"He's the one on the clocks," says Bella. "Did you know that? One day it'll be him who's giving the orders around here, not Judge Butterworth."

The warden with the notebook lifts it to his face and begins scribbling again. I wish Bella would keep quiet.

"Come on, Oswald, let's get on."

Bella strides up the slope in an obvious attempt to outpace the wardens. I follow behind her, looking back just once to see the old chaps struggling to keep up.

Ahead there are three cottages linked together, one door and one upstairs and downstairs window in each. Bella knocks and waits outside the first of the three. When there is no answer she tries the door and it opens. She steps inside. She leaves the door open for me and I enter a dark, cold passage. The ceiling is very low and there's a strong smell of something bitter. Turpentine, maybe. Bella has disappeared.

"Here," she whispers.

There is a door at the end of the passage and an alcove adjacent to it. Bella is standing just inside. She lights a match, and then a candle. She steps back.

Taking up the complete height of the alcove, which is taller than Dad and wider than Frank

Broadfoot, is an extraordinary machine. It's a clock, but nothing like any clock I have seen before.

The main clock has black roman numerals on a large silvery-white face. Above this is a row of three smaller faces and below, five pairs of dials. The clock, faces and dials are set into a black wood that I realize, as the flame illuminates it, is carved into a tangle of vines and leaves through which faces peer out. There are angels, devils, cloud faces, star faces, horses, birds and fish. There are rows of tiny panels and drawers set into the wood in no obvious arrangement.

"The clock has twelve working dials," says Bella. "And a mysterious thirteenth. This one."

She holds the candle nearer. There are three smaller dials above the main clock face. These have illustrations etched into them. The first is obvious, it's the sun; flames leaping from it, it shines down on a farmer in a field. The next is the moon, the third less obvious.

"Constellations," says Bella, without looking up from her duties. "Sun, moon and stars." She straightens up and looks at me. "Above those," she says, "look. The thirteenth dial."

~ FOURTEEN ~

At first I can't see anything. There's a white dial with what could be the maker's name etched in the centre. Then, as I look closer I can see what the fuss is all about.

I can make out two letter "O"s – but the first is smaller and the second is leaning to the right. Above this is what looks like an apostrophe. Together they form Oswald O'Connell's initials. So that's why they call me the one on the clocks.

"It could be anything, couldn't it?" says Bella. "But Mum has made up her mind. And she thinks it's you. The prophecy doesn't help."

This makes my heart sink. Another prophecy. The world is made up of people who want to see the future and those that think they can.

"I think it's all rubbish," says Bella. "And I think you and your dad are up to something. Remember, you can fool my mum, but I can see right through you."

I could put an end to all this now. I could just

tell her Dad made up the name O'Connell like he's made up hundreds of other names for himself. But she might think he did it to deliberately deceive everyone, and that won't help.

"Now watch carefully," she says. Bella opens a tiny door below the main face and inserts a key.

I try to follow everything she does. She opens hatches and tiny drawers. From her toolbox she picks out a pair of tweezers and then a fine brush. She dusts, polishes, oils a hinge here and there. She peers in compartments and using an extended finger nudges a mechanical element. Her fingers are quick and precise. Although I wouldn't want her to know what I'm thinking, I'm quite impressed by her skill.

Then suddenly it's over. She bends down, shuts the case and blows out the candle. She pushes past me, leaving me staring at the extraordinary timepiece. "So, there you are. Hope you followed it all," she shouts, disappearing out of the house.

I pull the front door behind me and try to keep up with her.

At the end of the row of cottages she makes a sharp right and sprints up some stone steps. And there, sitting on a wall at the top, puffing away, are the two ash wardens.

"The Judge certainly gets his money's worth out of you two, doesn't he?" says Bella, without slowing. As I pass them I keep my eyes on what's up ahead.

Cut into the hillside above is a small house surrounded by thick shrubs and a tangle of vegetable plots.

Bella approaches the dark entrance and knocks. Again she waits, then attempts to push the door. This time it doesn't give so she pulls a set of keys from her pockets and unlocks it.

The clock in Mill Lodge is identical to the earlier one. This one is in the hallway near a large window, so it's easier to see the detail.

Bella winds and cleans the clock. I stare at the thirteenth dial. It seems clear enough now. A small O, a larger sloping O, then a large, clear apostrophe. Oswald O'Connell.

For the rest of the afternoon I follow Bella obediently. The locations of each of the clocks are similar: small houses, or cottages, inhabited by people who are either out working, or who are reluctant to make an appearance. I don't doubt this has something to do with ash wardens.

Each of the clocks has the same inscription on the thirteenth dial.

I know it can't be me. I am not anything

special. I am certainly not going to take on Judge Butterworth and I need to make sure he doesn't think I will.

But if it isn't me, what is it? What are those strange circles on the thirteenth dial? There has to be some simple explanation.

Finally there is one last visit, to Clacker Farm, a long walk. It's on a tor squeezed between the Butterworth's proud estate and Hugh Blight's twisted spire of a rock. We skirt the Green for a short distance then leap a stile to cut across a meadow.

And at this point the ash wardens give up on us. They lean on the stile for a few moments and seem to be discussing something. Then they're gone.

Bella strides ahead but I hang back. The meadow is full of wild flowers, and although the day is overcast, sunlight seems to penetrate through the cloud and here and there a butterfly bobs into view.

And there it is, my favourite, the sulphurous brimstone, the one, Mum told me, that is the original butterfly. There was an entire case devoted to these in the City Museum. It wasn't a grand case, nor was it in a prominent position. But the fact that this butterfly had its own display gave it a status above the others. I thought then that its name wasn't right. It should have just been called "the butterfly". It's the colour of butter and makes me think of sunshine in a warm kitchen, on a summer's day, with Mum preparing tea. Calling it brimstone was cruel.

For a few seconds, now that the wardens have gone, I feel almost free. It's a sensation that doesn't last long.

"Oswald!" yells Bella from the other side of the field. "What are you doing?"

"Look at the butterflies!" I shout back, and realize immediately I shouldn't have said it.

"Butterflies?" she yells. "Butterflies? Are you an idiot? Come on, we have work to do!"

The brimstone dips away, fluttering off towards the Green. I watch it for a few seconds and feel like I'm saying goodbye to an old friend, then I turn away and follow Bella's trail through the long grass.

Another stile at the top of the meadow leads to a steep track between high hedgerows. There are brambles and nettles oozing a damp, hot stink. The afternoon is warm, and bees tumble out of the unnaturally bright ceiling of cloud and bury themselves in the mouths of vivid flowers. I see spiders building elaborate webs that span incredible distances. I spot another brimstone butterfly sitting on a cluster of drooping purple petals. I don't stop, but slow my pace to stare at it for as long as I dare. Bella disappears round a turn in the path, a deliberate ploy to make me keep up with her; she knows I would look even more stupid if I lost my way.

Clacker's Farm is dilapidated and beyond repair. Sheds and outhouses lie in ruins. Hedges are out of control. A few sheep chomp the grass on a bank behind the farm. A cow stands immobile, staring at us.

"I don't know how these people keep this place going," says Bella. "Mum thinks they must have ash hidden away somewhere."

In the yard a docile lamb and a peacock stand looking at each other. As we pass it the peacock begins to make a terrible noise.

"Hush, Caesar," Bella shouts. Miraculously, the peacock quietens.

We crunch across the gravel to the front of Clacker's Farm. The door is open.

A lanky, pasty youth steps out, a shotgun in his hand. His eyes are pale and watery and he has a large, purple bruise on one temple. "Mother's just been eaten by a fox," he says, his face registering no emotion.

I look at Bella, who seems amused by my shock. A little smile creeps across her face.

"'S'not funny," whines the youth.

"Sorry, Dryden," says Bella politely, "but Oswald here doesn't understand. He thinks it's your mother that's been eaten by a fox."

Dryden laughs, but his face doesn't. His expression doesn't change at all. "The mother of the chicks, only a few weeks old. Fox got her this morning. Hate the stinking thing." His voice is a shrill monotonous howl, as if it hurts him to speak. He stares at me, his fingers flicking nervously over the trigger of the shotgun. He grins. "So, Elizabeth thinks you're the one on the clock. Come to save us all, have you?"

FIFTEEN

I follow Bella into the house. Inside it is eerily dark. The front door leads immediately into a dank, warm room where curtains are drawn and a small fire flickers. An old woman, whom I presume must be Mrs Clacker, is sitting reading by lamplight in an armchair. It's the first time I've seen anyone read since I got here. She looks over her spectacles at us. She's a frail-looking woman, with white hair and a crinkled face. But her eyes are quick and intelligent.

"Is this the great Oswald?" she says, sniggering.

"Yes, Mrs Clacker," says Bella, "the boy who sees the future in his sleep."

"Oswald O'Connell," says Mrs Clacker, and she gives me a long, penetrating look, "you should be careful what you say. Some believe you are the destiny of Idlegreen! Some say it is you whom the clocks speak of." And then she sniggers again, a nervous, irritable laugh. "Bella was here winding the clocks the morning after your accident. She was very shaken up, I can tell you. Her mother thinks you are the one, and you talk of a new star!" Her face changes expression, as if she's choosing her words carefully. "Keep your ramblings to yourself, Oswald, unless you intend to annoy some very powerful people."

My eyes fall upon her book and she snaps it shut. She stands up and looks at me. "Do you like books, Oswald?" she asks. "Do you?"

She peers at me so intensely I feel trapped. The room around me goes very quiet. Bella is waiting for my reply as much as Mrs Clacker.

"Do you?" she says again.

For a moment I'm five years old and mum is sitting on the edge of my bed. She is reading me the story of the goats and the wolf.

"Do you like books, Oswald?"

It's as if I'm on stage and everything else is dark, just me in the spotlight. I want to speak but can't. I feel trapped inside myself. My pulse thumps in my head. I nod.

"I knew it!" she yelps. "I could see it in your eyes! He likes reading, I thought, as soon as you stepped foot in here." She drops her book on to the floor, grabs the lamp in one hand and gets to her feet. "Follow me, and see what wonders there are here." She brushes past Bella, ignoring her.

I trail after her into the passage that leads from the front room, past their clock, into a hallway with a wide staircase with long banisters.

She opens a panelled door and stands there, lifting the lamp as if discovering a great cavern.

"You see?"

I push open the door a little further to let myself past her. The room is cold, and there are huge heavy curtains drawn over what I presume is a tall window. In the centre is a large dining table. The rest of the room is lined with books. Hundreds of them.

"Dryden has never been very interested in reading," she says. "And I will never read them all. So, my dear boy, you help yourself. Come and go as you please." Mrs Clacker holds the lamp just below her face now, making her features sinister and ghoulish. She reaches out with one bony hand to touch me. "But in return, just do me one small favour."

I look at her and nod.

"Say no more about any new star. Please keep your predictions to yourself. You don't want to upset everyone, do you? Don't ask too many questions. Don't get too nosey. Keep your questions, your thoughts, and your nightmares to yourself. Then everything will be all right."

She narrows her eyes and cranes her neck so her face is next to the lamp.

"You don't want your father to be locked up for ever, do you?"

She's been talking to Butterworth. Whatever it is that's going on here, she knows about it, I'm sure of it. The look she's giving me is not just very threatening; it's desperate.

I smile weakly and, edging forward, squeeze past her and out of the room. I can sense her eyes following me.

Bella is waiting for me in the passage. She stands with her hands on her hips, her head tilted to one side. "Well, Mister Bookworm," she sneers, "since you know so much, you can do this clock yourself." She kicks the toolbox towards me.

This isn't a sensible idea. She has much more to lose if I make a mess of this. But, nevertheless, she stands back, folds her arms and leans against the wall. She indicates with a nod that Clacker's clock is my responsibility. So I begin.

The clock has to be wound, the faces polished, hinges and springs given a spot of oil, and the ornamental woodwork given a dust and a clean.

I kneel down and open the toolbox, searching

for the polish. I hear the library door pulled shut and Mrs Clacker walks behind me.

"He's wise to keep his mouth shut," she tells Bella. "Obviously a very bright lad."

"That's good," replies Bella. "Because he's looking after your clock from now on."

The labyrinths of the wood, the intricate twists and spirals, the leaves and branches and creatures that peek through need close attention. I try to lose myself in them. Bella says nothing, which I suppose is a good sign. Or perhaps she's hoping I'll make a mistake. I polish the faces, apply tiny drops of oil. The clock is like a living thing that needs care and attention.

I hear Bella's footsteps behind me as she disappears into the front of the house.

I squat down and begin wiping the columns of smaller dials. The top pair are slightly larger than the rest. They contain tiny painted illustrations of boats in harbour, and, I assume, must display the times of tides. In the centre of each of the smaller dials below these there is a tiny, detailed painting of a vegetable, a flower or a fruit. A single hand extends to the circumference, where, instead of numbers, there are minuscule illustrations of seeds, of plants in leaf and of pots and sacks.

I realize I'm deliberately avoiding the thirteenth

dial. I don't want to look at it. I don't want to see those initials again. Somehow, I hope that when I look at it now it will seem ridiculous to think the dial could mean me.

I move upwards, polishing, wiping, oiling. At last my eyes reach the dark triangular area of clock above the three dials of sun, moon and constellations.

There it is. And there is no doubting it.

o O'

And then a sudden whining, a grating, nasal voice, echoes in the passage around me, startling me.

"The lower dials are the sea and the land, the seasons of planting, growing and reaping." It's Dryden Clacker, although where he's appeared from I don't know. "Time, the sun, moon and stars exert forces beyond the power of human beings to control, they exist in a different realm, their influence is inescapable."

I turn to see him standing above me, his long, colourless face staring through me to the clock. I try to think of something to say, but his reedy voice continues with his sermon.

"And there's you, on the thirteenth dial." He laughs. "The destiny of Idlegreen." His watery eyes stare at the dial. He seems to be in a trance. He begins to recite some sort of verse.

"When he arrives upon the thirteenth dial,
on those who fortune has forsaken, now she smiles."

His face is expressionless. Then he turns to look at me.

"Haven't you heard the prophecy? Idlegreen has been waiting a long, long time." He begins blinking rapidly, as if waking up from a spell.

"There are twelve clocks, you know, not ten. That's what many of the older villagers say."

He steps closer, still far more interested in what he has to say than bothering to look at me.

"They are hundreds of years old. They once stood in cottages around the Green. They've long gone now, the cottages and the workers. But can you imagine, these poor families, in their tiny homes, with these great timepieces dominating their lives?"

Then, to my relief, Mrs Clacker's voice interrupts him.

"Dryden, what are you talking about?" I turn my head to see her standing at the end of the passage. She looks extremely nervous. "Leave that poor boy alone," she snaps, glaring at her son. "He doesn't want a history lesson."

By the time I'm done and begin packing up, Bella reappears. "Dryden wants us to go up to the top of the tor," she says.

"The cloud is clearing now," he says, his voice coming from outside, high-pitched and monotone, as if he can't be bothered to waste energy on the effort of speaking. "We could light a fire."

"All right," says Bella, with no enthusiasm. "We don't have to be back for an hour or so."

"Don't be long," Mrs Clacker calls after us. "And, Dryden, remember, don't talk so much." She cackles at her own remark, and disappears back into the house.

We trudge after Dryden, through the yard and up towards the summit of Clacker Tor. The low cloud, which has been with us for days, is breaking up. Above the tor patches of vibrant blue sky are visible. The evening is brighter than many I have known for weeks, and after only a few minutes' walking I am beginning to feel uncomfortable. The path to the summit snakes through a field in which the Clackers' cattle graze, or stare at us as they lugubriously munch the cud. For people who don't seem to do any work, the Clackers are making a good living.

The top of the tor is rounded and even, with enough grass to play a ball game, and, although dwarfed by Blight's gnarled outcrop, it has a breathtaking view of the sea. The sun is still above the sea and a narrow strip of blue sky sits along the horizon. Above this a vast, strangely luminous, bank of cloud is tinged with pinks and purples.

Before we reach the highest point of the mound there's a gentle hollow and evidence of other fires; it looks like Dryden spends many evenings up here. Perhaps he, like Butterworth and Blight, likes to keep an eye on what goes on.

He begins immediately, pushing stones and old bricks into a rough circle. He grabs a handful of tinder from an untidy pile of twigs and rolls of bark and layers it carefully in the centre of the bricks. He builds it up, throwing on larger and larger twigs and anything at hand. Bella helps half-heartedly, still holding on to her case, picking up the odd bit of kindling and dropping it on.

I've made enough fires for them to be a drudge and I'm far too warm to need its heat. It's obviously an amusement for Dryden, a boy who's nearly a man but who is never likely to leave this place.

From this angle I get a good view of the bruise on his head. "How did you do that?" I ask, pointing.

Dryden looks up at me, his mouth hanging

open. His hand moves up to the bruise and his fingers touch it, as if to remind himself of it. "I'm not allowed to tell," he says.

He returns to the preparations for the fire; there's a crackle and it's alight. Bella stands still, watching him. I sit at the top of the hollow overlooking them, hoping for a breeze to help me cool off.

"Looks like it's going to be a fine day tomorrow," he says, in his tuneless way.

"Don't expect to get much out of him," Bella says, but I don't know whether she's talking to me or to Dryden.

The flames twist and coil, spitting sparks. I follow one as it rises, majestically, into the warm air. I catch the hint of a breeze and stand to feel more of it. As I straighten up I realize the exposed strip of sky is considerably bigger and, as the sun drops down on to the horizon I see something that makes my legs give way from under me.

But Dryden turns, and is quickly beside me. He grabs me by the arm, propping me up.

"What is it?" he asks. I nod my head towards the horizon.

Following the sun down into the west is a bright green-blue radiance, a luminous comma. It's the new star.

"You shouldn't be surprised when your own predictions come true," says Dryden casually, "you should be proud!"

And I can hear Bella behind me, breathing noisily.

"Catastrophe," I hear myself say out loud, and I'm surprised by how hoarse and dry my voice sounds. "Catastrophe!"

Sixteen

The next thing I know I'm hurtling down the tor, into the narrow lane between the hedges. I can see Dad's mad, hysterical writing before my eyes, scratching the words across the sky.

"Catastrophe!" I yell, unable to keep it in my head. "A new star!"

I can hear him muttering and grinning – "Watch the skies!" He is ranting as his pen continues to scratch and the ink bleeds through the clouds – "Terrible danger!"

Then I'm plunging back through the meadow grass, trying to catch my breath, trying to shake his voice out of my head. It's not easy.

"Oswald!" I can hear, "Oswald," a voice echoing across the island. It's not Dad now, but Bella, calling from way behind me, her voice almost lost on the breeze.

Over a stile, then a bank and I'm stumbling across the lane on to the Green. The ground is hard and my feet hurt, but I keep going. The village is in the long shadow of Blight Tor, and looks unwelcoming and sinister.

"Catastrophe!" I yell, and the word bursts out of me like an explosion of steam from an engine. All the stuff I've bottled up, the strangeness of Idlegreen, the nonsense about being the special one, Butterworth's threats, the bewilderment that has kept my mouth shut for the last few days, it comes out in a stream of words I hear echoing across the island. "Watch the skies! Beware the new star! The destiny of Idlegreen!"

Nobody appears, not even an ash warden. But I know I am being watched. I can feel the telescopes and the binoculars spying down on me.

I sprint straight over the crossroads and into a lane that soon peters out and becomes a track twisting through the ruins of old cottages. I stop when I can't run any more, when my heart is beating so fast it might rip apart, when my head is such a jumble of voices I can't hear.

Somehow I've run across the island, right to the other side. I'm standing on a cliff path looking over the dark sea to the east, towards the sunrise to come.

And I have to stay here, because I want to see it in the morning. I don't want to hide from it. Dad told me to watch the skies. And if there is a new star he must have known something about it. Mother Fortune must be speaking to him. And now she speaks to me.

I don't know what's going on any more.

I bury my face in my hands and sob. I cry tears for me, for my mum, for my dad, for the madness that is everywhere.

I lift up my head and yell, "I am not the destiny of Idlegreen! I cannot see the future! Mother Fortune, you are the fraud, not me!"

Something scuttles through the undergrowth. It brings me back to my senses.

The evening is already chill, and even before night falls, I'm leaning against a rock, hugging my knees. I have to look for somewhere to give me some better shelter. But as the light fades, and the first stars appear, it gets so dark there is nothing to guide me except the silhouette of the tors and the sound of the sea.

Then, behind me, I hear strange sounds. I twist to look back round the rock, and on an expanse of cliff-top turf, now in almost complete darkness, I see dark shapes. Some are still, like molehills, others edge forward, then stop, then edge forward once more.

Trying to see what they are is almost impossible. The more I stare, the more they seem to defy remaining one thing; their shapes change, become larger, or flatter, or disappear completely. It's only when I remember the old trick of looking to one side, just off centre, do I recognize what I'm looking at. Rabbits, hundreds of them, using the cover of night to eat the lush grass on this heath.

And then right next to me, so close I can extend my arm and touch it, is a fox. I can hear it breathing. It turns its head, which I can only just see, and looks at me. Go ahead, I think, go and get your supper.

And so it does. It slopes off, soundlessly, towards its prey.

When I look again the rabbits have gone. The fox has scared them away, with or without feasting on one or two of them first.

I push myself up to follow the dark snake of the path. I can just see it. It's dangerous, but I'm not in the mood for playing safe. My foot catches on something and I trip, falling awkwardly. My chest crashes into a rock. I have an ugly, hot pain in my ribs and in my lungs. I roll on to my back and look up at the night. I close my eyes, and sleep.

I wake three or four times and the pain is still there. Each time I consider going back to the stores but then decide against it. I want to be alone at sunrise. If it is true, if the star is there,

Bella, and whoever else she has told, will think I have predicted it. I'll be treated as some sort of crazy soothsayer. I'll stay out here, on my back, staring up. The night will only be a few hours.

It is so silent out here. I hear nothing creeping around me, nothing stirring in the undergrowth. Once I hear an owl, but I'm so tired I just sleep.

The next thing I notice is the birdsong. And then the clear, blue morning sky.

For a second I glimpse the sun, and beneath it, rising above the sea, a smaller, greener star. But then my eyelids clamp shut and my eyes fill with tears. I try to sit up quickly but my chest still hurts.

I can't look again but I am certain now, it's there. A bright, new star.

I get up, but moving in any direction sends a shooting pain out from my ribs. And then I hear a voice, calling from a long way off.

This time I scramble to my feet, ignoring the pain. The light from the sky above the sea is harsh and bright, and already the morning is warming up. After so many overcast days, the light is eerie and unnerving. I cut back across the heath until I rejoin the path I must have taken last night. Above me, to the right, is Frank Broadfoot's windmill, dazzling white in the morning sun. I skirt the tor and soon have a clear view of the Green.

I make my way back slowly, painfully, the heat battering the back of my neck. I can feel the air shimmering and buzzing.

The voice again, nearer now, perhaps on the other side of the stores, on the lane. I see her now, it's Elizabeth.

I can't shout back because of my chest. I wave but she doesn't see.

"Oswald!" she calls out. She looks distressed. I feel guilty, and yet somehow touched that she's bothered to wonder where I am.

I get used to the ache in my ribs and break into a trot. Then, at last, she sees me. She waves, puts her hands over her mouth, then waves again.

As I come out on to the lane I can see she doesn't know what to do. She doesn't know whether to open her arms to welcome me, or to stand with her hands on her hips. She does both and then folds her arms, then starts walking towards me. She's wearing a coat over her nightdress. She looks like she hasn't slept all night.

Outside I'm shocked by how bleached everything looks, how everything seems drained of colour. There is an intensity to the light, to the walls, the reflections from windows, to the paintwork on doors and the flowers in gardens around the Green. Above the island, the sun and somewhere close to it, the new star, combine to create a vast corona of blinding white.

"Oswald?" she says, a question in her voice. "Are you all right?"

I explain about my fall.

"Bella told me about last night," she says. "We don't know what to say. Bella is quite upset. You were right, Oswald. You were right." She has that smile on her face again. The one that suggests she thinks I am the one on the clocks.

"No, it's not true," I try and explain. "I can't predict the future. It's not possible." I walk beside her slowly, walking is easy enough, but talking at the same time hurts.

Elizabeth suggests I go to bed for a few hours, that a rest will help fix the soreness in my ribs. That's exactly where I want to be but not because of the pain.

She follows me to my room with a glass of water and puts it on the floor next to the bed. I climb straight in and pull up the sheets.

"Yes, you were right, Oswald." She's smiling again. "You don't even know it yourself, poor boy. But you are the one the clocks speak of. You will restore our fortunes."

I definitely don't want to hear this. Sooner or later everyone else on the island will see this new star. Then my reputation will be confirmed. I'll be the destiny of Idlegreen. And Dad and I will be bound for Gull Rock.

SEVENTEEN

More voices in my head. Not Dad this time, different voices. Some chant, others mimic; there are factions, some are with me, some against. There are young ones, too, some very young, and these laugh and shout. I can hear their little feet running up and down. There's some sort of game going on.

I sit up in bed. The window is open and a cool morning breeze fills the room. The taste of ash in the air has disappeared. The potatoes have gone. The room is tidy, has been swept.

My chest feels sore but the sharp pain has disappeared. I pull open the curtains. The light on the back garden is so intense it's almost white. I look back into the room for a few seconds, but my eyes can't cope with this sudden contrast and everything blacks out.

I get dressed and make my way to the stores.

Now I can hear them. I move to the window next to the till. There's a small crowd at the crossroads. Some are sitting on the wall; others are standing on the lane.

Children are playing on the Green and I notice the dust that trails after their running feet. One of them is trying to fly a kite. Their cries echo over the Green but the gathering outside the stores is more subdued.

I stay in the shadow of the building, trying to see if I recognize any of them.

Standing in the lane are three men in working clothes and an old woman, I think it's Mrs Clacker. Then there are two or three teenagers, huddled together in a small group. Bella is there, talking to Dusty the postboy. In the middle of them is the scrawny tor pipeman, Hugh Blight, who is waving his thin arms towards the sky. Some of the others are looking up, following what he is saying. Some are ignoring him completely. Elizabeth is there too, standing with her arms folded.

Behind Hugh Blight is Wolfgang, the cab driver, his face pinched and sullen and, standing to one side, looking up with one hand shading his eyes and the other holding something in front of his face, is Frank Broadfoot, the big miller.

Two ash wardens sit further along the wall. I recognize them as the pair who followed Bella and me yesterday. The one with the glasses is watching carefully. The other, with the long beard, looks hot and uncomfortable.

I decide it's time to step outside, to see what's going on, although I think I've probably guessed.

Hugh Blight, his eyes darting everywhere, even as he's lecturing everyone else, spots me first.

"Aha! Here he is, the destiny of Idlegreen, the fortune-teller himself!"

I knew it would happen.

The teenagers and a few of the adults laugh at this, or rather at me. I'm squinting, not yet awake and startled by the light. The heat of the morning bounces off the lane; everything around me seems to shimmer.

"Oswald!" Elizabeth shouts as I cross the road, and immediately runs towards me. "Don't get upset," she says, putting an arm over my shoulder. I'm not upset. "They're not making fun of you."

Yes, they are.

"Here he is, ladies and gentlemen. The one who has come to bring you all good fortune." It's Hugh Blight again, cackling away at his own sarcasm. No one else laughs. I think it must be the look on Elizabeth's face as she walks beside me.

Bella is watching carefully. Her gaze isn't unkind: something's changed.

One of the teenagers separates himself from the group. It's Dryden Clacker, and he's walking over with his hand out.

"I would like to shake your hand, Oswald." His squeaky voice irritates me. "You knew this star was coming." Then he leans closer to me, as if he doesn't want anyone overhearing. "But you must be careful."

I shake his hand. It's limp and cold. His mother cranes her neck. She peers at me with pursed lips.

"Dryden, what are you telling him?" she squawks.

Bella approaches me and stands next to her mother. "You were right, Oswald," she says, squinting up into the sky above the stores. I turn to look. "But I don't think the Judge is going to like it."

The light is so dazzling it's impossible to keep my eyes open.

"Try this," says Frank Broadfoot, and he passes me a rectangle of black glass. "Go on, look through it."

The glass is thick and almost opaque. But when I hold it up to the sky I can see it, just as I had feared. A new star, rising above the tors, a short distance below the sun.

"Interesting, isn't it?" says Broadfoot. "And you

knew about it before anyone else. Astronomer, are you?"

I hand back the square of glass. I'm not sure what to think any more. "No," I croak, my voice still surprising me. "No, I'm not an astronomer." I check to see if anyone else is listening. They're not. "I saw it when I fell out of Wolfgang's cart. I just saw it before anyone else, that's all."

"And you think it's a portent of doom?" He takes a step closer to me. He is huge. As tall as Dad but thick set, too.

"No, I don't," I say without hesitation. "If I was an astronomer I'd know exactly what it was. But it's not a sign, or an omen, or anything else."

"Well, I'm glad of that," says Broadfoot, "because if you did think it was some sort of warning I'd think you were nuts."

And then an argument begins to break out between Wolfgang and Hugh Blight.

Elizabeth turns away, Bella follows her.

"The boy is no menace, Mr Blight," Wolfgang shouts. "What are you talking about? He can't help it if he has a gift!"

I go to step forward, to get a better view, but Frank Broadfoot pulls me back.

"He saw what was going to happen in the trap," I hear Wolfgang tell everyone who will listen. "On the day of the accident. The knock on his head must have given him special powers."

Hugh Blight is raising a long finger. "He is an outsider; he is meddling with our affairs. We shouldn't trust him! Perhaps he should join his father in the cell at Hook Head."

"We'll lock you up first, Hugh Blight!" It's Frank Broadfoot, his voice booming over me.

For a moment there is silence. Everyone is looking at the miller.

He puts his hand on my head. "Why don't we hear what he has to say? Shall we give him a chance?"

Now all eyes are on me. Then it's Mrs Clacker's voice that breaks the silence. "His Lordship is about to grace us with his presence," she says.

I notice one or two people start to brush themselves down, pat their hair. Hugh Blight looks distinctly put out, as if he had been enjoying his brief moment of command. The sound of hooves rolls across the Green and Butterworth's carriage comes into view, leaving a plume of dust in its trail. Some shield their eyes, as if in the presence of somebody more than human.

Frank Broadfoot takes his hand from my head. "The Judge will expect our full attention. Try not to stand out too much."

The horses are brought to a halt. The Judge pushes himself up and, as he does so, the carriage judders. The Judge stands and closes his eyes, deliberately giving us a moment to admire his flamboyant costume. He is wearing a gold coat embroidered with silver stars and a wig held in place by a large three-pointed hat topped with a colossal peacock feather. From one of his sleeves he pulls a large silk handkerchief. He dabs his forehead. His face is caked in pink powder and his lips are painted a vivid red.

"People of the Green," he says, his podgy face puckering and wrinkling, "today we are privileged to witness a spectacular celestial phenomenon." He raises an arm and flicks his handkerchief towards the sky. "However, I understand that there are silly rumours circulating in the vicinity that suggest this is some sort of sign, a portent of gloom and doom. I assure you, you have my word, it is not."

Well, not such an idiot after all.

"It is not a calamity, nor is it a disaster, no, no, not at all. Yes, it is a novelty to human beings here on earth, but it is certainly not a threat to our exalted isle. So please, return to your homes and do not be alarmed."

At this point there is some shuffling of feet, a few whispers.

Hugh Blight clears his throat. "We were celebrating, Your Honour."

A few voices murmur their agreement. The Judge looks puzzled. "If I thought it was the end of the world I would surely celebrate too," he says. "For what else would there be left to do?" He giggles at his own words. Then he adds, less pleasantly, "Where is the boy?" He shields his eyes from the glare and begins to seek me out.

"That'll be Oswald," says Hugh Blight, without hesitation, pointing in my direction.

Butterworth's piggy eyes eventually locate me. "Young man, I don't think you were listening to me the last time we met. Please do not upset the good people of the Green with your lunatic outbursts. This island is peaceful and well ordered. I have already warned you once, and I won't do so again." His expression suddenly changes. His eyes bulge, his lips draw back over his teeth. "If I hear anything more of your nonsense, you, your father and anyone else who pays attention to your balderdash will be left to rot on Gull Rock." He stuffs his handkerchief back into his sleeve and, after dropping his huge bottom on to the seat, instructs his driver to pull away.

People look at me from the corners of their

eyes. They turn their backs on me, or, if they are close, take a few steps away.

Frank Broadfoot is still behind me. "The Judge may look like a clown," says Frank, "but he is a shrewd and ruthless enemy. You will have to watch your step."

Suddenly I see Elizabeth and Bella looking unsettled. They scurry off towards the stores.

"Sorry," I hear Elizabeth say as she passes, "but there's work to be done. Let's get on." I see that forced smile again. Next thing I know Dusty the postboy is standing in front of me.

"Another letter for you." He grins. "Double nothing, you are," he says enigmatically. I try not to look puzzled, just nod and take it from him.

Then I realize what he means.

EIGHTEEN

Back in my room I sit down on the bed.

The envelope is similar to the last one but he hasn't used the typewriter this time, preferring to stick to his mad, yelling capitals.

O O
THE STORES
THE GREEN
IDLEGREEN

This is what Dusty meant by "double nothing". The initials. But Dad has turned them into a little doodle. He's drawn lines radiating out of them like suns.

He can't know about the clocks, so he must think this is some sort of joke. The doodle on the envelope is odd, but it doesn't prepare me for what is inside. There are six sheets but very little writing. Instead there are just scribbles. Arrows, circles, little stars and mad little exclamation marks and things like

CATaSTRoFE HERE!!

Then there are little calculations, scribbled out, numbers circled and underlined. I recognize a drawing of the world with the sun and the new star above it.

Most of the pages are filled with this sort of thing, all totally incomprehensible to me. Maybe he understands it, although I doubt it. It looks like he's really lost his mind.

I continue to stare at the letter, trying not to reach an inevitable conclusion. Even if Dad is released, which, judging by the look on Butterworth's face is unlikely, he'll never be the person I need him to be. I will be looking after him.

There's a knock on my door. I shove all the papers and the envelope under my pillow, then pretend I'm looking out of the window.

"Can I come in?" It's Bella.

She closes the door behind her and steps into the room. She looks at me, but when I catch her gaze she stares at the floor.

"Look," she says, standing at the end of my bed and fiddling with her fingers. "I haven't been very nice to you, have I?" Her eyes remain focused on the floorboards. "That first night, you were shouting so loud we could hear you throughout the house."

It's difficult to feel bad about something you can't remember doing.

"You were practically screaming, and screaming stuff about the new star being a warning." She puts her hands over her face for a few moments. "And it sounded so real, as if you were scared too. That was the worst thing." Now she looks at me as if she wants to make sure that what she says next comes out the way she means it. "Oswald, are you the one on the clocks?"

I'd like to tell her that Dad made up the surname, so it couldn't possibly be me. But that might make more trouble for Dad. I shake my head. "No, Bella. Double nothing. I'm a nobody."

She doesn't seem convinced. "Are you scared, Oswald?"

And when she asks that I want to tell her immediately that I'm not, that there is nothing to be scared of, that it's all just superstitious rubbish. But I just can't say it.

"Please say something, Oswald." Bella sits down on the end of the bed.

"What's there to be afraid of?" I say, which as

soon as I say it, I realize is just a way of not answering the question.

Bella sighs. It's a sigh of resignation, as if she shouldn't have expected to get a decent, straight answer. "What's there to be afraid of? Isn't it obvious? There's a strange new star in the sky. We can see it in daylight! You told us days before it appeared that it would come, that it would signal the fate of the island. It sounded like the world was going to end. Isn't that scary?"

"It's not true," I tell her. "I saw it before anyone else, that's all. And because my father thinks everything is a sign, because he's always making stupid predictions, I became muddled up. That's all there is to it."

Bella drops her head into her hands. She looks at me through her fingers. "Dusty told me you've had another letter. Does it tell you anything?"

"Only that Dad's losing his mind," I tell her. I take the letter from under my pillow.

I watch her leaf through Dad's scribbles. At first she looks angry, then just puzzled. She raises a finger to her eye to push away a tear. When she's finished reading, she looks up at me.

"You must feel so alone."

I can't look at her now. I stare out of the window and fight back my own tears.

"And now the Judge knows who you are," Bella sniffs, "he's watching us all the time. We have to be so careful from now on."

There's a sudden crash downstairs, and the sound of someone shouting.

"Isn't that your mum?" I ask her.

"I thought she was out," she says.

But the shout is Elizabeth, then there's another voice. It's Hugh Blight.

Bella leaps up and I follow her. She charges ahead of me, down the stairs, through the kitchen and there, standing in the storeroom, a pot under each arm, is Hugh Blight. Elizabeth is trying to pull them away from him. "You've already helped yourself once," she says, her teeth clenched.

"You owe them to me!" he shouts. "You haven't paid any of my bills for six weeks. Six weeks!"

Both of them look hot and glistening with sweat. Elizabeth hears us and when she looks up the fight seems to go out of her.

"And I'll be back for more soon," he spits. "This doesn't clear your debts, not by a long way."

"I hate you, Hugh Blight!" Bella screams, rushing towards him. Elizabeth holds her back, but she can't stop her daughter from yelling at the old man. "Do you think you can take everything?"

He stops, looks around the stores, then grins, revealing teeth stained brown with tobacco. "Well, there isn't that much left to take," he says.

Blight kicks open the door to the shop and casually saunters out. "That's enough," I hear myself snap. My head is exploding with rage, for everything he said on the Green this morning, and now for this. I follow him to the door and watch him head off towards his farm. I want to chase him and punch him, but suddenly I have a better idea. "Hugh Blight!" I shout. "Hugh Blight! Are you listening to me?"

He turns and stares at me.

"Beware the thirteenth dial! You cannot ignore the thirteenth dial!" I'm beginning to sound like Dad.

He turns and glares at me, and despite the noon heat, his face is grey. His mouth hangs open. "What do you know about the clocks?" he gasps. I keep my eyes fixed on his and say nothing. Then he turns, and hurries away.

NiNETEEN

There is rebellion in the air. I've lost count of how many people have warned me about the Judge. And yet, although I know how careful I should be, the next day I get the exciting first scent of mutiny on the Green.

I had been perched up on the stool for an hour or so, dipping the pen and writing in the ledger. A few customers had come and gone, we were introduced and exchanged nods. But when the Hope sisters appear, something changes. It's the way they look at me.

The Hope sisters own the tor that stands on its own towards Hook Head. They have a vineyard and make their own wine. There are a few bottles of theirs on the shelves and have pretty hand-written labels, no two the same.

Diana and Miranda – they look a lot older than Bella but younger than Elizabeth – come in giggling. They fill the room with their youthful smiles and laughter; one of them is singing, the other tapping a beat on the shelf with her finger. Bella immediately comes down from the ladder. She doesn't do that for anyone else, I've noticed.

They stand in the far corner, chatting and occasionally looking over at me. They have their hands over their faces, as if they've been told something they can't quite believe. When Bella imitates their hand movements, their expressions and their laughter, she looks like she could be their younger sister. But there's a slight madness to her behaviour, an edginess that covers up a deeper worry.

Which is understandable, I suppose.

I remain slumped on the stool, flicking through the pages of the ledger.

And then, at last, Bella moves over towards me. She places her splayed hand on the broad pages to get my attention. It's quite a friendly, jokey sort of thing to do, encouraged, without a doubt, by the sisters' incessant sniggering. I can't turn the page, nor read it. I have to look up.

"Well," says Bella, staring at me, an "I know something you don't" look on her face. "Well," she says again. "Guess what?"

"Let me think," I reply. "I know. You've discovered a colony of unicorns living on the island."

She's a little taken aback by this. She turns to the sisters. "He's become really sarcastic since he started speaking. I think I preferred the strong, silent Oswald." She looks back at me, a little trace of amusement in her eyes, as if she's enjoying this game. "No," she says slowly, "nothing to do with *me*." She puts a big emphasis on that last word.

"Right, I get it." I look at her, then across at Diana and Miranda, who stare at me with a look of disbelief. I'm a sort of talking pet, I suppose. A curiosity. "You've realized, at last," I tell her, "that I'm really king of the jellyfish. Is that it?"

"No, no, much better than that." She shakes her head. "Hugh Blight is frightened of you."

I am lost for words.

The sisters begin laughing again. Now Bella has shared their secret there's no reason to hold back. Their laughter is so loud it rattles off the shelves of bottles and jars.

Bella raises her voice to be heard. "He was seen running from here yesterday. He met Wolfgang, the cabby. He said you told him something it was impossible for anyone to know. He said you'd put a curse on him."

I can't help it. I grin. I want to maintain my composure, to try and pretend that there is something wild and mysterious about me. But it's impossible. "Good!" I shout. "That's really, really good! It's what he deserves!"

The sisters' laughter goes on but now they're clapping their hands and jumping up and down, as if they've been waiting for this moment for years.

Something has changed. Rather than being afraid of Blight, they are ridiculing him. And if Blight can be made a figure of fun, why not the Judge? It isn't impossible.

After they've gone I feel elated. Bella is suddenly serious.

"What did you say to him?" she says. I tell her about the thirteenth dial. "It just popped into my head," I explain. "It surprised me when I said it."

"And what's so strange," says Bella, a puzzled grin on her face, "is that Hugh Blight doesn't own one of the clocks. Why would that bother him?"

But this is just the beginning.

News spreads fast – I am the wizard who has cursed Hugh Blight. I am the fortune-teller who predicted the coming of the new star.

Towards the end of the day the number of customers calling into the shop suddenly leaps up. Each buys a single item and, as I note down the transaction in the ledger, starts asking me questions.

"What crop will yield the best returns this year?" asks one.

"Butterworth's Bank has offered me twenty pots of best ash for first refusal on this year's harvest of potatoes. What do you think?" asks another.

"Will my daughter visit me this summer?"

"How long will this dry spell last?"

I do my best to answer without offering them false hope. I measure my words carefully.

"I expect you will receive some news soon," I tell them, or, "I think we can safely say the best is yet to come!"

Inhabitants of the Green who haven't set foot in the shop for twenty years turn up, cash jingling in their pockets. If they were once wary of being watched, by Hugh Blight, or by the wardens, they aren't any more.

There are three of them now, permanently perched on the wall opposite the stores like three wise monkeys. They look uncomfortable and miserable. The buttons on their scarlet uniforms flash when they catch the light from the sun, or from the new star, and their black hats are tipped forward to shield their eyes. They look hot and fed up.

Bella makes sure no customer leaves empty-handed. No one is allowed to approach the counter unless they have at least something in each hand. They will take anything, just as long as they can ask me something.

Mr Sugar, holding a bottle of vinegar, asks me whether his onions would win the "Best in Show" rosette this year.

"Your onions are unbeatable," I tell him. His smile was worth the fib.

"Mr Sugar," says Bella, "Mr Sugar hasn't been out of his house since his wife died! And he's just bought all the salted fish. All of it! And he says he'll be back tomorrow!"

Elizabeth comes home to find us exhilarated. She stares in wonder at the gaps on the shelves. She has been out most of the day trying to pay off some of her debts but one glance at the amount of stock we have shifted makes her realize her problems could soon be over. For the first time I see Elizabeth's genuine smile.

Things are looking up. That afternoon, as each customer approaches the counter, Bella looks over them at me, her eyes wide with encouragement. She wants me to lie; I can see it. She wants me to make things up.

I can do that, if I have to, if it improves the atmosphere around here.

A showdown with the Judge can't be too far away.

TWENTY

And then pandemonium.

Early the following morning I meet Bella in the kitchen. She is dressed but looks startled and a little dishevelled. I notice she has nothing on her feet.

"Mum's had to go out," she says. "And she'll have a shock when she returns." She signals to me to follow her. "Try and keep quiet," she whispers. "I think there's a queue forming outside the door."

"A queue?" I repeat, exasperated. She nods. She puts her finger to her lips.

"I think," says Bella softly, "they came with Wolfgang in the early trap this morning. News has spread to Hook Head!"

And sure enough, when she takes me up to her mother's room to peer out, we can see a line of heads, none that I recognize. If they want their fortunes told I won't tell outrageous lies, I'll tell them what they want to hear.

The three wise monkeys are shuffling across the Green towards the stores, the buttons on their jackets aren't done up properly. One isn't wearing a cap.

And when Bella unlocks the door at seven thirty, and the queue traipses in, she directs them to the shelves, encouraging them to buy "specialities" of the Green and items that are in "great demand". These she had selected just twenty minutes before as worthy only of customers from Hook Head. She has quickly increased the prices on all of them to at least twice the original. "Thank you," I hear her say, and, "Much obliged," and, "Yes, he'll be here shortly, please be patient."

She'd asked me to wait in the storeroom; said that my presence in the shop would distract them from their purchases. And so, when I receive the signal, a short rap on the storeroom door, I take up my position in front of the ledger.

by Mr William Partridge of the Gables, Hook Head, three jars of Idlegreen Summer Fruits 6s 9d

Mr Partridge wants to know if his sister will be well by Christmas.

"Once we get to the New Year," I say, "her health will no longer be a concern."

by Ms Jayne Hawks of Bayswater Mansions,
Hook Head, a box of Supreme Candles 8
shillings

I tell her she shouldn't worry about her silly mistake. Nobody will ever find out.

by Mrs Grace Fleming of Quay Street, Hook Head,
four bottles of Hope Sisters' wine £1 4s 8d

Mrs Fleming asks me if I felt it was time for her family to leave Idlegreen and start a new life on the mainland. After seeing the exorbitant price Bella has attached to the wine, I feel Mrs Fleming deserves a long, detailed answer. I describe to her life on the mainland, the pleasures and the miseries of the city, and she is extremely grateful.

"You should stay here," I tell her, deciding, eventually, not to mince my words.

As the morning goes on, the early visitors from Hook Head begin to leave. I watch them drift across the road and gather on the Green, where they sit and squint at the new star, waiting for Wolfgang to return and take them home.

But there is one more customer: the ash warden with the white beard.

He places three bottles of ale on the counter and asks if they can be opened. Bella obliges.

"Thirsty work, sitting out there," says Bella.

"Wretchedly hot," he replies, grabbing the trio of bottles by their necks. "And hideously boring." He takes a step towards the door and then stops, as if he's just thought of something. "The Judge has been in Hook Head these last couple of days. He'll be back later." The warden lowers his voice to a whisper. "He won't have missed what's been going on here. We don't want to make trouble for you, but you can't keep anything from the Judge."

Bella locks the shop at lunchtime and, after she has run her finger down the ledger, announces this is the best day's business she can ever remember. For lunch she makes us scrambled eggs and opens a bottle of "Fossett's Original Lemonade" to celebrate.

In the afternoon, things continue much the way they were in the morning. Wolfgang brings another trap, full of the curious from Hook Head. Elizabeth had squeezed in among them and, when she appears in the shop, is red faced and so excited she can hardly contain herself.

"Bella!" she exclaims when she realizes what's

going on. "What did I tell you? Can't you see? He is the one on the clocks! Look what's happening!"

Bella shakes her head, although with a little less conviction this time, I notice.

Elizabeth runs from the kitchen, through to the lane, carrying trays, plates and bottles. She makes a few extra shillings selling biscuits and cakes to the anxious and the hopeful. She hums and sings, smiling at me with a tilt of her head. "Only six allowed in the shop at one time," she tells them as they shuffle forward. "You won't be waiting long. Why not keep cool on the Green with a glass of something refreshing?" She even hires out rectangles of smoked glass that Frank Broadfoot has left for us. "Examine the new star without damaging your sight," I hear her shout.

The ash wardens have found shade behind one of the cottages. Elizabeth takes them another three bottles of ale. On the house, of course.

Bella scuttles in and out, pushing overpriced items into eager hands.

Despite the overwhelming heat, Wolfgang continues to bring wagonloads of passengers from Hook Head.

I don't look at them when they come in. I don't want to encourage them. I just keep my eyes on the ledger. They place their items in front of me, I note them down, I take their money and ring it up on the till. I answer their questions, and bid them good day.

"You're the fortune boy, aren't you?" whispers an old man, leaning eagerly over the counter.

A girl a few years younger than me puts a penny on the counter.

"Tell me what I will do when I grow up," she says.

"Ride horses," I say, without thinking too much about it. "Live in a treehouse and eat ice cream." I put her penny back in her hand.

"I love horses!" she exclaims. "And ice cream!"

Most accept what I say; some need more.

I get to understand them just by their hands and the way they place their items on the counter. Old people grip cans and bottles, young people push biscuits and cakes towards me with their fingertips. I answer their questions. I don't look them in the eye. How can I? I don't like these lies, and neither will the Judge, when he finds out.

Now someone comes in and, instead of following Bella's instructions, choosing something before approaching the counter, this mysterious customer just stands there. I can't look up to confirm this but, in the corner of my eye, there's a tall, dishevelled character. I think he has a red beard, and he's staring at me.

I pretend to be checking the sales, my finger travelling down the page, and look as if I'm adding figures. But he's still there and has taken a step closer.

Bella would normally distract a customer who did this. She would draw them over to the vinegar, or the pickled onions. But something seems to have gone wrong with our system; there are too many customers in the shop; it's so busy she hasn't seen what's happening.

Even without looking up I can tell there's something desperate about him. He is panting, as if he's been running, and I can smell the sweat coming off him. He has a bag clutched to his chest, and this is rising and falling with his breathing.

"Oswald," he whispers. "Are you all right?"

It's Dad.

TWENTY-ONE

He looks jubilant and is grinning insanely.

"Come on," he gasps, "we have to go!"

He still hasn't been noticed.

He drops the bag on the floor, lunges over the counter and grabs me, dragging me across the ledger, which I catch with my foot. It slams to the floor. Dad swings open the door, grabs the bag, and with me under an arm, runs out into the lane.

Now there is a commotion from the shop.

"He's been taken!"

"Abducted!"

"Stop them!"

I follow the faces of people in the queue as Dad bounces past them. They haven't yet realized what is going on.

Dad runs round the side of the stores and away from the Green. He sprints across the backyard and up the path to the cottages on Mill Tor, then leaps over a tumbled-down stone wall and into a cabbage field. He drops me then grabs my hand.

"Come on, come on! Let's go. Run," he hisses, "run!"

"I don't know," I mumble. "Bella and. . ."

I want to tell him about the stores. I can't just leave them now. But he's in no mood for sense, I can see that. His eyes are wild and his face is contorted with a lunatic intensity. I want to hit him for being so stupid. But I want to hug him too. I want to hug him and tell him how much I have missed him.

The field slopes up to a line of trees. He pulls me with him, scrambling over a broken wooden gate and, gasping for breath, we drop behind a big old oak. Dad cranes his neck to look down the hill to the stores.

"Ha! They don't know what to do! They aren't used to such daring! Such an undertaking requires surprise. And, Oswald, they look quite surprised."

I can hear shouts and peer round the tree. Light is reflecting off the roof of the stores; I block it with a hand. Some of the customers have spilled out into the lane. Now the queue is alerted it begins to break up. Some are dispersing over the Green, others are simply bemused and stare at each other. A few are looking up towards us, but not with the certainty you would expect if they knew exactly where we are hiding.

Then there is panic.

The first thing I notice is the dust cloud. It rises from above the cottages and moves towards the stores. The crowd scatters, screaming.

Three horses thunder into view. It's the Judge and his sons. The Judge has a riding crop raised. "Where is the convict?" he hollers. "Who knows where he is?"

The sons dismount and disappear for a moment. When they return they are pushing the three ash wardens before them. "Dozing, all of them," one son yells to his father.

The Judge, still in the saddle, steers his horse towards them. "Useless old fools!" he screeches. They cower and cover their heads. "Which way did they go?" The Judge is furious, almost out of control. But, despite his demands, no one seems to know which way we've gone, or are not telling.

Then he drops down off his horse, elbowing one of the wardens out of the way and strides towards the stores. His sons follow.

Someone screams. I hear Elizabeth pleading with him. There is the unmistakable sound of the shelves crashing down, of glass shattering and splintering, of windows smashed.

The crowd has scattered now, only the ash wardens are left, huddled together and frightened.

Bella and Elizabeth appear in front of the stores, holding each other. I need to help them.

I try and pull away from Dad. I want to go back. He grabs my wrist.

"Nothing you can do, now," he says.

The Judge comes into view, his sons behind him. He climbs up on to his horse. "You're finished!" he yells. He waves his crop at Bella and Elizabeth, then swings it towards the wardens. "All of you!" The Judge swipes at his horse, and in a confusion of hooves and dust, the Butterworths disappear across the Green towards their estate.

Dad's grip is hurting now. I try and wrench my arm away, but it won't come.

"What can you do now?" he says. "Just listen to me, will you?" He lets go of my wrist, opens his bag and takes out two apples. He passes one to me. "You see, I was right. Look at the skies now. We have two or three days, that's all." His eyes are distant, as if he's obsessed. "And then boom!" The sound reminds me of the ledger slamming on to the floor of the shop.

"I need to go back," I tell him.

He takes a huge bite from his apple. "No, no, we've got to get away from here. It's our only hope."

"They need me there. Please, let me go back."

He stares at me. His new beard gives him a slightly demonic look. "Don't you understand? Haven't I made it clear?" He puts his hand on my arm. "My dear, dear boy," he sighs. "I think the end is nigh."

"What?" I grab his hand. "What are you talking about?"

"I told you to watch the skies, didn't I? This is clearly an omen of catastrophe. You got my letters? Didn't you read them? Isn't it obvious what I'm talking about? I told you this island was too blessed. Its fate hangs there, above us." He points into the harsh light above the Green. I look up for a split second, but the light is blinding, making my eyes sting and water.

I put my head in my hands. He seems so brittle now, so close to complete madness. I have to be careful what I say. I want to run to the stores, help them sort things out, find a way of fighting back. I was beginning to feel I could belong there. But what will happen to Dad if I leave him now?

The pressure of my hands on my eyes sets off a swirl of colour. Then an after image appears, a ghost of what I have just glimpsed above the Green. I couldn't see it when I looked directly at it, but the pulsing echo of it swims before my eyes. I see a spiral, a twist of feathery greens and purples.

I've seen pictures of something like this before. It isn't a star.

I take a deep breath.

"Dad," I tell him, "it isn't a new star. It isn't an omen." My realization comes as such a relief I can barely bring the word to my lips.

"It's a comet!" I say at last.

Dad is dismissive. "You can call it what you like. I call it Mother Fortune's revenge." He takes another huge bite from his apple. "She is heartbroken by the way her signs have been ignored!" He munches noisily. "We have to get off the island, my boy. Idlegreen is doomed, maybe the whole world. This place has been too fortunate and its people too full of greed and love of possessions. It couldn't last, just couldn't last."

He doesn't know what he is talking about. Elizabeth and Bella own next to nothing, they are hardly full of greed.

"And I am a hunted man, so it's not going to be easy." He looks at my apple. "You going to eat that?"

I shake my head. He takes it and crunches into it. Then he suddenly looks distracted.

"The Judge. He came to see me yesterday. He

stood and stared at me through the bars of the cell door. He stared and grinned. His fancy clothes and his stupid wig. 'Mr O'Connell,' he said," and Dad pretends to be Butterworth, twisting the strands of his wig, pursing his painted lips. "'Mr O'Connell, you are obviously guilty. But we will have to have a trial, just for a demonstration of what happens to criminals. You can expect ten years, Mr O'Connell.' And what was worse, Oswald, he went on to describe the dungeon he wants to transfer me to! It's a cave! A damp, dark hole on some lonely rock! For ten years! I wouldn't survive ten days!"

Dad takes one more bite of the apple and throws it into the air. I can't follow it because of the light, but I hear it whistle up. It drops down just behind us, I turn in time to see it smash on a rock and explode into fragments.

"So, when Smedley's back was turned, I just walked out. He never bothered locking the cell."

I have to ask him something. "Dad, when you gave me the name Oswald O'Connell, you didn't know something, did you?"

Dad laughs. "I didn't give you that name. I just called myself Jeremiah O'Connell. That was the name of the brute who owned the brush factory I slaved in. First name that came into my head." He puts his hand on my back. "You shouldn't read so much into things, Oswald," he says.

"So what do we do now?" I ask him.

Dad grins. "Remember what I've always told you, Oswald. Mother Fortune will look after us."

Dad is barely sane, and now he's Idlegreen's most wanted man. Somehow, I think, it will take more than a sign from Mother Fortune to get us out of this one.

TWENTY-TWO

We scramble around the back of Mill Tor, Dad ignoring my protests. The steep slope with the white windmill on the summit gives us some respite from the glare. We slump down on to a pair of rocks that sit at the base of the tor, overlooking the sea.

"I need to go back, Dad," I tell him. "I can't just leave them." He looks at me blankly, as if he can't remember what I'm talking about.

"Elizabeth and Bella. They rescued us, they've looked after me. They need me there to help them. I can't just abandon them."

Dad shakes his head. "I can't believe what you're saying. Go back and then what? Are you mad? Don't you understand anything? This island is doomed. And you will be too if you don't come with me."

I want to pick myself up and run back to the stores. I want to tell him that he's wrong. But he's so close to the edge of madness I dare not say a word.

"We'll have to lie low for an hour or so. They'll be searching for us," Dad says, as if I couldn't work that out for myself.

The sea is behind us and is eerily calm. A fishing boat gently bobs on the water and seabirds glide over, enjoying the gentle breeze. How can catastrophe strike now? It looks all so peaceful, so quiet.

Dad can't be right. I refuse to believe he is right.

I follow him anyway, along the side of a narrow wheat field, and then back up towards the mill.

We come to a small shelter dug into a bank. It seems to serve no purpose other than a place to sit and look at the view. This is part of Frank Broadfoot's place. I can imagine him sitting here on a summer's morning, a mug of tea in his hand, smiling to himself, looking over his fields and the sea.

"We can stop here," says Dad. "I have some things for us to eat in the bag, but we'll need to stock up soon." He drops the bag on to a long bench, then cranes his neck round the shelter to look back at the mill. "I'll do a quick sortie in a minute," he whispers. "This place looks like it could be well stocked."

"No, Dad!" I say it with such force he looks bewildered.

"What do you mean, no?"

"You mustn't steal from him, or anyone. You can't. I know the man who lives here. He would help us if he could. He's not a bad man!"

Dad looks a little taken aback, then his face breaks into a sarcastic mockery of mine. He repeats my words in a squealing, pleading voice. "Oh no, Dad! They are nice people! We must starve, Dad, because the big, fat, rich people around here are sweet and kind!" He glares at me. "They don't care about us! We are nothing to them! What's the matter with you? And anyway, there probably aren't enough days left for them to eat what they've got in their larders. Think of it, a juicy ham, a pork pie, some delicious raspberry jam on freshly cut bread!"

"You're a thief, Dad. And what's the point of food if there are only days left to live?"

I regret saying this immediately. His face crumples. He drops down on to the bench, hanging his head. He motions for me to sit down next to him.

"Yes," he says, after a pause. "I am a thief. I admit it. How would you have survived without me?"

Without him I would still be at the stores.

Without him I could have a future to look forward to.

"You say this bloke in the mill is a nice chap," he says, without looking at me. "Well, if he is, why not go and knock on his door and ask him for something to eat?"

I'm just about to despair of him when I realize this isn't such a bad idea. Frank Broadfoot wouldn't turn me away. And it might prove something to Dad.

"All right," I reply, and his face lights up. "I will. I'll go and ask him."

"That's my Oswald," he cackles, and rubs his hands together.

The shelter is just below the level of the top of the tor, and from it the mill and the adjoining house are in clear view. A path of flagstones leads all the way from here to the back door of the house, almost inviting me to go and knock.

"See you in a minute," I tell him and without giving myself time to think about it, set off along the path.

Frank Broadfoot answers the door. He wears an apron. A haze of flour surrounds him. "Oswald!" he booms, wiping his hands down his front. "How nice to see you! Fine weather we're having!" He looks past me to the garden, then looks puzzled.

"Why have you come round the back? Are you lost?"

I tell him about Dad.

He shakes his head. "I'll be done for harbouring criminals," he laughs. "Do you want to come in?"

"We better keep moving, the Judge will be sending out search parties."

"Right," says Frank. "Just hang on a minute." He disappears back into the house.

I hear a whistle and turn to see Dad squinting round the shelter. I hold up my hand, trying to signal that I'm all right. Beyond him the sea merges with the sky as the afternoon heat pounds down on the water.

"Take this," says Frank. He holds out a basket. It's full of bread rolls. I can see some cheese and some fruit. "There's a cold chicken underneath," he says. "Eat that first."

I take the basket and hold it in both hands. "You're very kind, I'll never forget this."

He looks a little embarrassed. "Never mind that," he says. "Now, I don't know what your plans are, but between here and Morden Tor there are some deserted cottages. You could stop there until this blows over."

"You think this new star will just blow over?" I don't understand what he means.

"You don't really think. . ." And he begins laughing. He takes a step towards me and puts a hand on my shoulder. "You don't really believe your own midnight hollering, do you?"

He's right. I'm not a fortune-teller. I don't know what is going to happen. It's impossible to know.

"No, our biggest worry right now is Judge Butterworth. You're going to have to keep your heads down for a few days, then try and get off the island." He suddenly looks over my head. "I think your father's getting impatient."

I look back to see Dad beckoning me to hurry up. His eyes are wild and staring. The red beard doesn't make him look any calmer.

"Thank you for these," I tell him. "I hope we don't get you into trouble."

"Butterworth is a big shot on the island, but he won't mess with me! Off you go, and good luck!"

I nod and turn away, then take off across the path back to the other side of the lawn.

"What were you doing?" hisses Dad. "Talking about old times?" He sees the contents of the basket. He stares from it, back to me, then looks over to the house where Frank is still standing at the back door. Dad rummages into the basket, prods the chicken and discovers some biscuits. It's obvious he can't believe someone could be so generous. "Why did he give you all this?"

"He wants to help us, that's all."

Dad narrows his eyes. He looks across at Frank and this time gives him a very restrained wave of thanks. "We've got to get going. Give me the basket. You carry this." He hands me his canvas holdall, which is so light it must be almost empty. He grabs the basket.

"This way," I tell him, and we head off, down the back of the tor, towards the cliff path I can see snaking ahead of us.

"I hope you know where you're going!" Dad yells.

"Away from here, for a start," I call back. "I know somewhere where we can hide out."

When we get to the cliff path I slow down a little. Dad immediately overtakes me to set a faster pace. With Mill Tor behind us there is no shade, the heat is almost unbearable.

"We must move as quickly as we can!" he shouts, a little breathless himself.

I find it difficult keeping up with his giant strides without running. The path is narrow and overgrown. I catch my foot in a bramble, leap a clump of nettles and land on an uneven stone, jarring my ankle.

Eventually Dad slows a bit and I get a chance to look down to my left, where the bank falls away and disappears over the cliff edge. Mill Tor is behind us now and the path cuts through a ribbon of scrub between the cliffs and a wheat field to our right. Ahead is the island's most southerly rock, Morden Tor. The cliffs are more treacherous here; ahead I can see where they fall vertically from beneath the route of the path. Below us there's a cove, a beach of sand and pebbles, still glistening from the sea.

Looking across the wheat between the tors I can make out Butterworth Tor. The Judge's mansion looks like a Greek temple, bleached white and radiant in the scorching sun. His farm is a vast network of hedges and a patchwork of crops. Workers, like ants, crawl over it, pruning, picking, filling carts, making money for the illustrious Judge, the pompous clown.

A solitary cloud wanders across the sky and, for a moment, I imagine it's the Judge, his fat, painted face pouting and grimacing. Wisps of vapour, like powder from his wig, lift off the cloud and fall away.

Suddenly Dad stops dead in his tracks and I almost crash into his back.

"Well, well," he says. "I think we may have been given a sign!"

Not another sign. Mother Fortune is obviously still with us.

He puts one hand on my back and, standing next to me like a great sea voyager, he holds an outstretched arm, indicating the first glimpse of a new world. Just below the horizon, shimmering like a mirage, is an island, and just beyond, another. Further north, following the sweep of his arm, is a lighthouse. The Craven Lighthouse.

"It's not that far back to the mainland," he says. "We'll find a way!"

It doesn't occur to him that we don't have any means of getting off Idlegreen. I think of suggesting the Evans' boat, but decide against it. I can imagine posters of him on every wall in Hook Head. If we go anywhere near there, he'll soon be back in his cell. Far from getting concerned about any of this, Dad is excited.

"Think of the tales we can tell. What adventures we have had!" And then he turns his face up to the sky and starts shouting. "Mother Fortune, you have not forgotten us! We will build a monument to your sagacity."

And then, as the path begins a gradual descent into a shallow hollow between two jagged peninsulas, I spot the cottages.

"A haven!" Dad cries. "Don't you see, Oswald, how at every turn our luck seems to be changing?"

I don't have the heart to tell him I was just following Frank Broadfoot's directions.

"And look, a stream!" he hollers. "We have food, shelter and fresh water! We will yet escape this doomed island!"

It's not Idlegreen that's doomed. It's us.

TWENTY-THREE

The cottages are derelict. But there's enough roof on one of them to give us some respite from the heat. They were probably fishermen's cottages once. The stream cuts between them and then breaks in several directions, flowing a short distance down a chalky slope to a beach. There are few traces of the occupants who, for whatever reason, deserted their homes.

Dad begins clearing away a space, marking his new territory with the holdall, the basket and his grey prison jacket. He disappears for a few minutes then returns first with large rocks, then some driftwood. He sets up a little dining area and begins to clear a space to build a fire.

I watch him building a neat pyramid of tinder and straw. "Do you think that's sensible?" I ask.

"It'll get chilly later, we must be prepared!"

"Won't the smoke send out a signal, show where we are?"

He thinks about this for moment or two, then

shakes his head. "We are in good hands, now, remember?"

I don't ask him to explain the mechanics of that. How Mother Fortune will prevent our pillar of smoke, rising into a cloudless sky, from being noticed by the Judge and his men. I turn away.

The beach looks like no one has set foot on it for years. I amble down to the water and watch the waves slide in. I have the beginnings of a normal life here. We have no home on the mainland; we had to leave when Dad stopped paying the rent. I don't want to go back to the thieving and begging he calls "the entertainment business".

I want to stay on Idlegreen. I want to stay here and help Elizabeth and Bella fight back. Butterworth isn't invincible. Dad's wrong about catastrophe, wrong about everything. He's messed things up enough, and it's time I put a stop to him, or Mother Fortune, deciding what is best for us. Neither of them has a clue.

I'll have to tell him.

We dig into the chicken and the rolls, eating in silence. A gull lands on the exposed beams under an opening in the roof and watches us.

"Dad. . ."

He raises a hand to stop me, fishes in his holdall

and pulls out an enamel beaker. "Property of Hook Head police station," he scoffs. "I just want to taste the water in the stream." He hops over the basket and disappears. I can hear him singing as he goes. The seagull takes off.

I think he knows what I want to say to him. Perhaps I should just forget about talking to him. Perhaps I should just go.

I spot Dad standing in the stream, signalling to me. At first I think something must be wrong, then realize he is pointing to the sea. I follow the line of his finger and there, just off the tip of the next headland, moving on the ocean, silhouetted against the brightness of the waves, is the outline of a man, hair thrown up behind him. He's walking across the water.

TWENTY-FOUR

"We mustn't get seen." I urge him inside the ruined cottage.

"But this could be a way of getting off the island!" Dad protests. "Look! He's walking across the sea! We could do that too!"

From a deep rectangle in the wall, where once there must have been a window, we watch the mysterious figure, and realize he isn't walking but just standing upright, his arms and legs splayed, as if trying to keep his balance.

"Do you think he saw you?" I ask Dad.

"He wouldn't have seen anything, would he? The sun is too bright."

"Both suns are too bright," I mutter.

"Yes," he repeats, "both suns are too bright!"

The figure is moving across the waves, parallel to the beach, bouncing on the water.

"He's standing on something," I exclaim.

"Yes, I thought that," says Dad. "Maybe he's

tamed the Great Worm and is riding upon its back. I've heard of such things!"

"There's no such thing as the Great Worm, Dad." I keep my voice down, pretend that I'm stating the obvious. "It was a basking shark," I tell him.

"What was?"

"That thing that came after us in the sea. It was a basking shark. I remember the stuffed one in the City Museum. They're big, but harmless."

He looks insulted. He clenches his teeth and narrows his eyes. "We escaped," he pauses and takes a long breath, and bellows, "from the Great Worm!"

The worm rider, or whatever he is, seems to be turning now and heading back the way he came. He is a little nearer now, and we can just see the shape of the thing he's riding. It could be a fin, but I refuse to believe it's the fin of anything living. I'm convinced he's floating on nothing more than a plank of wood.

He disappears behind the headland and Dad shrugs. "Well, we'll never know now, so I suppose," and he looks at me accusingly, "it's just a matter of what you believe!"

"I believe," I shout, without thinking what I am saying, "I believe you don't really care about me at all. If you cared about me you would take me back to the Green. I was happy there, didn't you notice? Did you even ask me if wanted to leave? Did you bother?"

He doesn't answer me, but turns away from the window and slumps down on the floor, leaning up against the wall.

"I think we better stay here tonight," he announces after a pause. "Light a fire, get some more of this food inside us and be up early tomorrow, try and find a way off the island."

I don't want to listen to him. I wish I could just run straight back to the Green.

"Come on," I hear him say. "Let's have a competition." He's looking at me in a way that suggests he's sorry. I think he knows he's not a very good dad.

We play throwing stones into the beaker. This game goes on for far too long, as games usually do when I'm winning. Dad refuses to accept defeat. Then I think something I don't want to hold on to for too long. I wish Bella was here. We were just beginning to get along.

"What round is this?" Dad asks.

"Round seven," I tell him. "You said it was first to five."

"No, I didn't, I never said five."

We can only begin something else when he wins, or I concede it was close and therefore it must be a draw.

When it's cooler we play tennis using two bits of driftwood and one of the trusty ping-pong balls from his holdall.

When I've long lost count of the points and given up trying to convince him I won a long time ago, he announces that the great beach tennis championship has been declared a draw and it is time for the contestants to shake hands and prepare supper.

I get the fire going with the matches Frank Broadfoot put in the basket and begin toasting the rolls. When they're hot, I'm going to slip a slice of cheese inside.

The rolls are soon gobbled up and followed by slices of sponge cake.

Afterwards, when we are ready to sleep, the fire is built up and a slim chimney of smoke escapes through the derelict roof. The sea stirs in the distance, a soft, hushing lullaby. But watching the smoke makes me nervous. Just to convince myself there's no one around who could spot us, and to scan the horizon one more time for worm riders, I move towards the open doorway.

And as I do, I hear a voice.

"Dad?" I call out. But it isn't Dad. Dad is snoring.

I'm frozen to the spot, trying to work out if there is another way out of here when footsteps crunch just outside. The next moment there's someone standing in the doorway.

TWENTY-FIVE

"Oswald?"

It's Bella.

"Bella!" I call back. "Yes, it's me."

Dad stirs but doesn't wake.

Her face appears in the entrance, illuminated by the glow of the firelight. She's wearing black: a black cardigan, buttoned to her chin, a long black dress and black boots.

"Camouflage," she says. She slips a heavy bag off her back. As she lowers it to the ground she sees Dad sleeping. "I'm very pleased to see you!" she whispers and kneels down beside my wheat mattress.

Dad stirs again, but this time he wakes. "Who's there?" he shouts, even though he should be able to see both of us quite clearly.

"It's Bella, Dad."

"Who?"

"Bella, from the shop."

Dad struggles to sit up, opens his eyes wide and stares at her. "What do you want?" he says.

"I've brought you some things," she says, undoing the straps on her bag and pulling out brown paper bags and neatly wrapped parcels.

Dad watches Bella for a few seconds and then announces, "We don't need your help, thank you. You may go!"

I can't believe he's saying this.

Bella pulls at one of the parcels before dropping it into my hands. It unravels to reveal a large cube of white cheese. "Look what she's brought, Dad!" I hold it up for him to admire. His expression is fixed.

"We have everything we need," he declares. He climbs off his bed, stands up, brushes himself down and stares hard at the collection of items Bella is beginning to arrange upon the floor. "We don't need anything, thank you!" he says again, looking from the assorted groceries to me, to Bella and back to the groceries.

"Dad," I try to keep my disbelief from getting the better of me, "even if we find a way off the island, we're going to need food for the journey."

"We can fish," he says. "I am a master fisherman."

Bella is still putting the final touches to her

arrangement. There are a couple of jars of something, a chunky piece of cold beef, a large loaf, a big bag of apples, some string, matches, candles, two bottles for water and a small canvas bag of tools. She's thought of everything.

"No, Oswald, we don't need any help. Now, Nelly, pack up and go."

"Bella," she says, "my name is Bella, not Nelly."

"Good for you," Dad spits back. He looks at me. "Well, Oswald, three's a crowd. If you want to stay with Bella then I'll be off." He tugs his hat out of his jacket pocket, it's crumpled and misshapen. He pulls it hard over his head and begins to walk towards the door. Pieces of wheat stalk cling to his back and trousers. He looks like a scarecrow. "Goodbye!" he says, and just as he disappears into the darkness outside he shouts back, "Hope you enjoy the end of the world!"

I can't believe he's doing this. I jump up, tell Bella not to move and chase after him. He hasn't gone far, about three steps and has stopped dead. There, hanging over the island is the eye of the comet, a brilliant swirling tail arcing behind it.

Dad is mesmerized by it. Then, after a few seconds, he whispers, "Look at it! Doesn't that thing chill you to the bone?"

I grab his sleeve between a finger and a thumb. "Come on, come back inside, please."

"No, we must go now. We must move by night. We don't have time to sleep!"

"What about Bella? You can't treat her like this. She helped us, remember, she saved us, she's looked after me!"

He scratches at his beard, then, although I can't see his eyes in the darkness, I feel him glaring at me. "How did she know where we were? Who else knows?"

Bella's voice comes from the doorway. "Frank Broadfoot told me. I asked him where you had gone."

"How did he know?" Dad cries. "We were directed by Mother Fortune." He lowers his voice. "Does this Mister Broadfoot communicate with her too?"

"What are you talking about?" says Bella, a little too bluntly.

I have to tell him the truth. "Frank Broadfoot told me how to find these cottages."

"Ah!" Dad declares. "Then he definitely communicates with Mother Fortune. Obviously a very intelligent chap. He hasn't told anyone else, has he?" he barks. "You don't think those worm riders are watching us, do you?"

"Worm riders?" says Bella, the smallest suggestion of a laugh in her voice.

"We saw someone out on the sea," I tell her. "Dad thinks it was someone on the back of a dolphin, or big fish of some sort."

"He was riding the Great Worm!" Dad raises his voice. "It wasn't a fish!"

Bella takes a few steps towards us. "He was on a bark," she says.

"What?" shouts Dad. "On a bark? What do you mean?"

Bella thinks for a moment. "There's a sort of settlement of bark riders who live on the beaches south of here. They are sons and daughters of farmers whose land was taken by Judge Butterworth. When their parents left the land to work in Hook Head, their children formed their own colony."

Dad swivels round. "You mean they can ride on the sea?" I can hear the excitement in his voice. "Well, if they can ride the waves, like the one we saw, then maybe they can help us get off the island!"

"Well, I don't think. . ." Bella realizes she has built up Dad's hopes.

"Could they get us off the island?" I whisper.

"They only ride the surf, they don't go out to sea." But it's too late.

"You must take us to them!" Dad shrieks. "Now! Come on! Now!"

Bella sighs. "You can't walk the cliff path at night," she says. "One wrong turn and you'll plunge on to the rocks."

"Mother Fortune will guide us," says Dad. "Don't worry about the rocks!"

TWENTY-SIX

I watch him walk off into the darkness. Perhaps this is the best way. I am not tempted to chase after him, nor call out to him. I will let him go.

The comet is still visible above the horizon, but its light doesn't seem to penetrate here and everything is soon reduced to inky silhouettes. Bella stands beside me. She reaches out and takes my hand.

And then I hear Dad again. "Even Mother Fortune's signs cannot be read in such darkness!" he calls. He stumbles back towards us. Bella lets go of my hand. "Perhaps it is her way of telling us to stay here until morning."

Soon he is settled in the cottage and snoring happily again. Relieved, and slightly exhausted by his madness, Bella is looking up at the night sky. She points to the swirl of gold, green and violet light now sinking behind the dark tors of Idlegreen.

"It's a comet, Bella," I tell her. "Did you know that?"

She shakes her head, then frowns, as if remembering something. She sits down on a rock next to the stream.

"I've been walking with it behind me for most of the afternoon," she says. "Every so often I stopped to look back at it, but the sky was far too bright. Even so, as I was tramping along the cliff path a tune came into my head. A sea shanty about gold in the sky."

I can hear her humming a melody under her breath. I sit down next to her and, in the last of the light, I see her turn to look at me.

"Dad used to sing it to me." She is staring at me. I can see she's trying to remember. "King Curlymane," she says eventually.

"What?"

"Dad learnt it from one of the old fishermen."

"The comet is called 'King Curlymane'?"

Bella pauses. She closes her eyes. Then she begins to sing. Her voice is low and quiet.

"King Curlymane has fire in his hair,
A nose that is frozen and a menacing glare."

Then her voice breaks.

"But that's all I can remember of the words," she says after a pause. "Except I know there's something about gold in it. Gold in the sky, like there is now." She sniffs again. "I wish the words would come back to me."

She goes very quiet. I know what's wrong. I need to say something. I can't see Bella's face clearly but I can tell she's listening. "My mum woke up one morning and said she felt dizzy. Dad didn't think it was serious and suggested she went back to bed. He went off to work. I went home in the middle of the day to see if she was all right. I made her some lunch and she said she was feeling better. But when I got back in the evening the doctor was there with Dad and one of the neighbours. She had died that afternoon. The doctor told us it was her heart."

"I remember saying goodbye to my dad for the last time," says Bella. "He went off for days on end, with the rest of the crew, on long fishing trips. Sometimes they came back with a boatload of catch, sometimes with nothing. He came to my room and sat on my bed. He said, 'Look after Mum.' And I hugged him and said goodbye. And that was it. I never saw him again."

"We've lost so much already," I say. "Perhaps it really is the end of the world."

TWENTY-SEVEN

In the morning the whole of the eastern sky is lit up, a brightness that is beyond the visible. It can be sensed by the skin on our necks, from the dark heat penetrating the backs of our heads. Our shadows are thrown ahead of us; they are vivid, sharp silhouettes that appear to be trying to escape us.

Bella looks like she's been awake all night. Her skin is pale; she looks anxious.

Soon, however, with Dad striding ahead like the great explorer he thinks he is, she gets a chance to speak to me.

"I need to tell you something. Just as I was leaving yesterday Sergeant Smedley came into the shop. He helped us put things back together after the Judge smashed the place up. Smedley told us the Judge had ordered him to pull together a militia to search the island. He doesn't want you getting away."

"Why didn't you tell me this last night?" I reply, horrified.

"Well, any brigade won't leave Hook Head before today and if I had told you last night you'd probably be dead on the rocks by now."

I see what she means.

"Come on, come on, come on," yells Dad. He is desperate to get to the bark riders.

"Oswald," Bella says as we reach a headland, "will you come back to the Green? We need you there so much. Remember the queues? As soon as they realized you'd gone, our customers vanished into thin air." She's quiet for a moment. "But it's not that. It was fun having you around."

"And what about the Judge? What happens when he sees I'm back?"

"We'll have to make sure you don't draw too much attention to yourself."

"Good," I say, "because I wouldn't come back to tell fortunes. I want to come back because I feel like it could be my home." I watch her closely then nod towards Dad. "But look at him. How long do you think he would last without me?"

She shakes her head. "And I hope Mum is managing without me. She's going to do the clocks today," she says. "But she hates it, especially when she has to go up to the Clackers'."

"I can understand that," I say, "they are a bit odd."

"Mum thinks Mrs Clacker hits Dryden. Do you remember he had a bruise on his face last time we saw him? He always has some sort of suspicious mark on him. Mum thinks Mrs Clacker does it."

"Is she crazy too?" I ask her.

"Mum thinks she's trying to stop Dryden telling us something. That's why she hates going up there. She thinks the woman is evil."

"Can't she just stop going?"

"We can't stop doing the clocks. It's something our family has done for generations. And I know it sounds terrible, but we need the money. Oswald," she continues, "we've made enough in the last few days, just from the shop, to keep us afloat for a few weeks." She grins. "Especially from the wealthier residents of Hook Head."

"They won't be back in a hurry, will they?" I tell her. "Not when they peel off the new price stickers and find the old ones underneath!"

She stops walking and grabs my arm. "We're not crooks," she says, looking at Dad. "We didn't rob anyone."

"No, but you were happy to go along with a deception."

"Well," she says, lowering her voice, even though Dad has moved quite a way ahead of us, "maybe it wasn't a deception. Maybe you can see the future. Maybe you are the one on the clocks!"

"Look," and I should have told her this before, "my name isn't Oswald O'Connell. Dad changes his name all the time, and I have to go along with it. I'm Oswald Smith, ordinary Oswald Smith. So the letters on the clock are nothing to do with me."

Bella puts her hands to her face, as if this has upset her.

"Don't tell me you were beginning to think I was your destiny too?"

"No, it's a relief," she says. "But I was beginning to think. . ." She looks at me steadily, taking both my hands in hers. "Look, I'm glad you are just you. I am, really."

Dad has stopped. When Bella and I catch up with him he's standing at a fork in the cliff path. One direction leads along the headland, a bare, exposed heath. The second path rises across a long, low hill, then on, I imagine, to the far south of the island.

He cups his hands round his eyes and attempts to look up at the sky, which, on any other day, I would think of as serenely blue. There isn't a cloud. He looks out to sea where the islands we saw yesterday are already lost in an impenetrable heat haze.

"Which way now, Nelly?" he says. "Where are the riders of the Great Worm?"

"My name is Bella," she says flatly. She stops beside him and looks up at him. "And they are not riding worms. I'm not sure where they are exactly, I've never been here before. I know they're along the coast somewhere near here."

I pick up a rock and, when I get the chance, fling it over Dad's head into the loose scrub. A bird squawks and breaks its cover, spiralling up, first flapping towards us, then turning away and heading off to the south.

Perfect.

"A sign!" shouts Dad. And he picks up speed and bounds up the path on to the slope of the hill.

He is so utterly predictable.

"He really thinks the comet is a warning, doesn't he?" whispers Bella. "So was the gloom and doom stuff all your idea or his?"

"His," I tell her. "I don't believe a word of it. Anyway, it's worse than that." I wait until she's walking next to me, so Dad won't hear. "He thinks it's going to crash down upon Idlegreen as a punishment for your greed and selfishness."

"What, mine?" laughs Bella.

"No, I don't know. He hates anyone who has

more than him." I look back towards the Green, but the last of the tors still obscures it. "And that's just about everyone, I suppose."

"And what do you think, Oswald?" she says.

"Don't know," I tell her. "I trust my eyes. I read books. I try and think scientifically."

"Oh, there's clever," she says. But I think she's impressed, at the same time.

When we reach the brow of the hill, an astonishing view lies ahead of us. Dad drops his holdall and stares, open-mouthed. Bella swings her bag off her shoulder and takes out one of the bottles of water. The land falls away before us, dropping down to a strip of golden sand that extends along the edge of the island into the hazy distance. The sea shimmers and sparkles.

"The wild south coast," smiles Bella, passing me the bottle.

Dad gasps and gapes, but it isn't because he's overcome by the beauty of what he sees. "There's nothing here," he says, his voice barely audible. "Nothing."

Bella moves up beside him. "Wonderful beaches," she says.

I squeeze in and place the bottle between them. Bella takes it. She holds it out for Dad, but I can see a telltale twist in his mouth. He wants to explode.

"I don't want beaches!" he roars. "I want worm riders!" He stares at her as if this is all her fault. "Why have you brought us here?" he cries. "Is this a trap? Have you brought us here to be snared like a couple of idiot rabbits? Lost your voice, have you, Nelly?"

"Dad," I push between them, "she didn't. . ."

"You've gone soft in the head, Oswald," he seethes, spit flying out of his mouth. "Don't you see what she's doing? She's probably getting a fine reward from that fat dandy Butterworth. Aren't you, girl? Aren't you?" He's spluttering now, dangerously angry. "Where is Butterworth and his little army? Behind that rock? On the beach? Yes, that's it! They are all down there, waiting for us. And they have a boat. And when we get there we'll be bound up, thrown in, and transported to some barren rock to perish!"

"Dad," I keep myself as calm as possible. "Bella didn't bring us here. You did. You chose the way, not Bella. Remember, just now, the path divided into two? You saw a sign, you said it yourself."

He looks from me to her, then back to her. He looks down to the beaches. They extend in the distance, broken into bays and coves by headlands, but one main strand is a great crescent of white, deserted sand.

The heath rolls away below us, and is overgrown with long, tough grass. Poppies grow in clusters, and there other wild flowers, ones I don't know, bright yellow ones. The path continues into the grass but stops there. Without looking back at us, Bella disappears into it, up to her waist, before I decide to follow. Dad has said nothing but is soon tramping down behind us, muttering away.

I try to catch up with Bella but she is moving ahead deceptively fast.

And then she stops and looks down to the beach below us. She turns back to us, a smug little smile on her face. I think she's found something. When I catch up with her I realize what she's discovered. There's smoke rising and, just detectable, the sound of voices. "Your dad will get on with these people," she says.

Dad is catching up with us and is either too hot, or too angry to speak. Then suddenly his mood lifts and he's happy again. "Yes! Yes," he yells. "Yes! Yes! Yes!" He pushes between us and runs on to where the path turns sharply, beginning its descent down towards the beach. He's looking into the sea, where waves are rolling and breaking before they slide up on to the sand.

He turns and grins up at us. I look beyond him, into a patch of water that is a bright translucent green. Riding across it, arms and legs splayed to keep their balance, are three figures similar to the one we saw yesterday.

"The worm riders," Dad hollers. "There are more of them! We can ride the worms home! I always knew! I always knew!"

TWENTY-EIGHT

One by one the beach people turn to stare up at us, breaking off from what they are doing and shielding their eyes against the brightness of the sky. They watch us zigzag down the steep, sandy cliff towards them.

The climb down is easier once we are in the cool shadow. Dad suddenly picks up speed but soon tumbles and lands awkwardly in a clump of emerald green parsley. Bella and I take an arm each and pull him up. To my astonishment, a swallowtail, possibly disturbed by his fall, is sitting on Dad's shoulder.

It's a large butterfly, and one the museum curator told me was almost extinct. It looks like an ink blot folded into two, but has an unusual outline, with striking wing tips. Either side of its body are two orange dots, like ghoulish eyes.

Two orange dots, twin suns.

"What is it?" Dad shouts, flinching. "Is it poisonous?"

"It's a butterfly, Dad," I tell him. "Just hold still." I touch the tip of one of its wings and it takes off, circling Dad's head, before fluttering upwards until we lose sight of it.

"I hate butterflies," says Dad. "You can't eat them, can you?"

Closer to us, a small team of workers lift their tools to greet us. One woman holds an axe aloft. She wipes her forehead with the back of her arm, then turns to hack branches off a log.

There are three of them in the sea, four or five playing some sort of game on the wet sand, throwing what looks like a small, stuffed bag at each other. A black dog races between them, barking and slobbering. A big group of at least twenty people sit on the sand at the entrance to a huge tent made of driftwood and old sailcloth. They look like they have been stranded here, happy survivors of a shipwreck. Their clothes are no more than rags, their skin deeply tanned, their hair long and knotted and tied up in various ways, with ribbons or string. There are other, smaller tents, sun-faded pastel greens and pinks, strung out along the top of the beach, close to the cliff.

A small fire smoulders away, untended. Scattered around it are pots, pans and plates, some in sloppy piles, some looking as if they've been thoughtlessly discarded. Others are stacked neatly, as if waiting for the next meal.

Dad is exuberant. He starts to race up the beach, tearing off his clothes, as he if has immediately recognized some kindred spirits and is eager to be one of them as soon as possible.

"Dad!" I yell at him. He turns and looks at me, impatient to join the others. "I'm not coming with you!"

Dad squints at me, then cups his ear to signal he wants me to repeat what I've just said. I take a few steps towards him.

"I'm not coming with you, I'm going back with Bella."

Dad looks confused. Behind him, one of the wave riders splashes up the beach, carrying his long, narrow bark under his arm. The wood is smooth and polished and sparkles in the sunlight. They are not riding worms, of course they're not.

Dad's white, bony ribcage is exposed to the sun, his jacket and shirt dumped between us on the sand.

"If you go back," he splutters, "you will be on the island when the sky falls in. Don't you understand? Why is it just me? Why is it only me who can see the danger?"

"Well, Dad. Maybe not everyone thinks there is danger."

"You could be wrong," Bella tells him.

"Wrong? Wrong? Me? Wrong?" His eyes are huge. "It isn't me who you are calling wrong. It is Mother Fortune herself! Oh, for goodness' sake." He glares at me and then at Bella. "Didn't he tell you about how she has helped us? The seabird, the weed, the miraculous escape from the . . . from the. . ."

"The Great Worm?" I add.

"Yes and the Great Worm!"

"It was a basking shark, Dad. I told you."

"And what about the new star?" he says, his hand waving towards the sky. "I suppose you think that's just normal, just natural. Sort of thing that happens everyday!"

"It's a comet, Dad. I've read about comets. People in the past, they all thought they meant something. They didn't exactly agree what they meant but that doesn't matter because the thing is. . ."

"It's just a comet," says Bella.

"Just a bit of rock, or ice, or whatever." I have to keep going now. "Just flying around in space as they have done since the world began."

"But Mother Fortune has led us here, to a place where we can escape this doomed island."

I look across at one of the bark riders, cutting across the surf, his arms outstretched. "You won't cross to the mainland on one of those, Dad," I tell him.

"It'll probably take you until doomsday just to stand up on one of them," adds Bella.

Dad raises his eyebrows. "Is that supposed to be a joke, Nelly?"

"My name is Bella," she tells him. She turns to look at me. "You want some sort of normal life, don't you, Oswald?"

I nod.

"Well, you're not going to get it with him," she says. She walks off, towards where the path meets the beach.

"I'm going now, Dad," I say, with as much conviction as I can muster.

Dad looks at me, then back to the people on the beach who are standing and staring, wondering what we are doing.

"You know," he says quietly, "it would be quite possible to make a bigger bark thing. One for two, or three of us." He elbows me playfully and, using his hand like a blade, slashes the air. "Whoosh," he says, "straight across. Home!"

"Dad," I say, after a short silence. "I am going back to the Green."

Dad says nothing. He doesn't explode, he doesn't rage or fume. He tries to peer up into the intensity of light above us but recoils and covers his eyes with two hands. "Mother Fortune," he whispers, "cannot tolerate such greed. This island is a lure for the worst instincts of humanity. She has led these people here to wipe them out!"

"But what about Bella and Elizabeth? They have next to nothing!" I'm astonished he can take his ludicrous beliefs so far.

Dad rolls his eyes. "They're just unlucky, that's all," he says.

"And why did Mother Fortune bring us here?"

"She didn't, our boat was sunk by the Great Worm!" His eyes are fixed, as if he has been hypnotized by his own ridiculous convictions. I turn and look at Bella. She is halfway up the cliff path and staring down at us. "I think we have two days at the most," says Dad. He bends down and picks up a handful of sand, then sifts it through his fingers. "It's very close now, the end is near. I'll stay here and see if I can learn to ride one of these things. If I manage it, I'll be back to get you. If not, well. . ." He sighs and looks at the sand falling from his fingers, his voice trailing off. "Yes," he says, eventually. "You can go back with Nelly."

"Bella, Dad, her name is Bella."

"Bella," he says, at last. He puts a hand on my shoulder. "You're a brave lad," he whispers.

"Dad," I say, "if you don't manage to find your way back to the Green, then I suppose we better say goodbye, just in case."

"I will come back to get you, Oswald. Have no fear, I will not let you down!"

For all his madness, I have to admire his optimism. I give him a hug.

"You have to know, Dad, that I think you're wrong about the comet. It will pass over us. It isn't a sign."

He nods. "I realize you want to hope for the best. But it is a father's job to be realistic."

I sigh quietly to myself. "I'm certain I'll see you again," I tell him.

He looks down at me, and is trying to work out how to respond. He's always been good at wriggling out of tricky situations, usually to get into even trickier ones, but now words fail him. I take his hand, and hold it for a while. Then he suddenly grabs me and hugs me again.

"I love you, son," he says.

"I love you too, Dad," I tell him. And it's true. I do love him, even though he's a bearded, batty fraud, a liar, a cheat and full of nonsense.

"When you see me again, I'll be able to get up on that timber and skate across the water. You'll be my passenger, of course. Mark my words." I shake his hand. "Goodbye, Oswald," he says.

I turn away and walk towards the path to join Bella. When we get to the top of the ridge I look back and give him one last wave.

Then I take a deep breath and follow Bella in the direction of the Green.

TWENTY-NiNE

"He really believes the island is in the path of that thing, doesn't he?" asks Bella, squinting in the harsh, eye-watering light.

"He believes too many things," I answer.

She listens as I recall our recent adventures. The string of islands, the gangs that chased us, the mobs that hurled abuse at us. I describe the last of the conjuring shows, how he stole a fisherman's boat, the incident with the basking shark, the gatekeeper's sixpences and then the apples.

Bella doesn't comment. But I can guess what she's thinking. With a record like that, Dad deserves to be locked up. I want to ask her about Elizabeth.

"Does your mother still think I'm the destiny of Idlegreen, the one on the clocks?"

"It's been difficult," says Bella, walking ahead of me. "At first I tried to convince her you were a fraud. But when things started to change at the shop, and we began to trust you, she started to think you were special in some way, some sort of lucky charm."

"Is that why you came to get me back?"

She stops and turns to face me. "I don't think you're a fraud, Oswald, not any more. My mum's been happy for the first time in ages, and that's why I like you, but I don't think you're the destiny of Idlegreen."

We have to keep our eyes on the path for most of the journey. The sky is a blanket of white heat.

Exhausted we come to the derelict fishermen's cottages, the place where Bella caught up with us. We stop for some water and for respite from the glare. From the shelter of the cottage we look out over the sea. We watch a lone bark rider twist on the waves.

And then we begin the long walk back, following one of the old sheep trails over the cliff tops. It's too hot to speak, so we press on in silence.

At last we drop into a vale that slopes down between Morden Tor and, further ahead, Frank Broadfoot's place, Mill Tor. If it wasn't for the dazzle of the twin stars we might well be able to see the Green from here.

But it's just as we're skirting Morden Tor that we realize we're heading into a trap.

"Look," says Bella. She spots them first.

Across the vale, trampling through a walled field that runs along the foot of Mill Tor below us, there is a line of red coats, twenty, maybe more. Leading them, astride a horse, is none other than Judge Butterworth himself. And beside him, on foot, I can make out another uniform, a dark-blue one. It's Sergeant Smedley.

Bella immediately crouches down, although there's nowhere to hide. "I don't think they could have spotted us," she says.

I drop down next to her and study them.

"So Butterworth has got his little army," says Bella.

We stay still and watch them trail across the field, then cut back, tracing a route that follows the foot of the tors. I watch as Sergeant Smedley, just a black speck, opens a gate to allow the Judge and his troop of ash wardens through. Smedley closes the gate and scampers back up the line to march beside the Judge's horse.

Then something happens that makes my heart sink.

It is obvious now what they're doing. The line stops again and we can just about see Judge Butterworth signalling to two of the wardens. The pair are left at the entrance to the vale, and are probably armed and able to signal to the others.

"He's putting a cordon around the island," Bella whispers. "He's not going to let your father get away."

"We better get moving, then," I tell her. "We'll need to cut over this tor and across the south of the island, then back to the Green before he can put his men there."

Without any further hesitation we're scampering up the side of Morden Tor, heading at a steep diagonal, hoping that the heat of the day slows the Judge and his warden platoon.

"The Mordens have lived here for generations," Bella explains as we cut across the farmyard on the summit of the tor. "We see them occasionally, but they haven't got a penny. Butterworth bought their good ash from them years ago. Waited until they were too desperate to argue."

We come to a line of old barns, barely still standing. Weeds push up through soil littered with small, jagged flints.

Suddenly there is a sharp clang and something whistles above our heads. A gang of crows takes off. At first I'm confused, then I realize it was a gunshot.

"Run!" yells Bella, glancing back. "As fast as you can. Run!"

Another shot, this one exploding in some mud ahead of us.

"The Morden brothers, up there."

There are two of them, sitting on the edge of the roof, passing the gun back and forth between them. Another shot hits a tree to my left.

"Those boys will shoot at anything," says Bella. "Don't take it personally."

We get behind the barns and try to work out a way down the tor and out of the sights of the gun-toting brothers. The most direct route is through a line of trees which would, at a rough guess, probably lead us straight into the path of the Judge.

I can see Bella is figuring this out as well. "If we're going to get ahead of Butterworth," she says, still trying to catch her breath, "we need to go that way." She points along the track that runs down from the farmhouse towards the centre of the island. There isn't any cover. We would be sitting targets. "It's your decision," she says.

"Through the trees. No choice. Let's go. If Butterworth and his army are there before us we'll just have to. . ." But I don't get to finish my sentence because the sound of two or three dogs, their ferocious barks echoing against the farm buildings, sets my heart racing and my legs ready to run. Both of us take off and head towards the trees.

Another shot cracks the air and hits the oak ahead of us. I realize the brothers can still see us through a gap between the barns. And there are the dogs to think about now.

We hurdle a broken fence and plunge into the trees. Immediately the land falls away and we find ourselves careering down through brambles and fallen branches, leaping precariously over boulders but somehow keeping upright.

At the far edge of the wood I can see a stream and then a sloping field. At the bottom of this, bleeding through a hedgerow like blood through a tattered coat, is an unmistakable line of red. Butterworth has cut off our escape.

THiRTY

Bella points through the woods to a bridge. "That's our last chance," she says. "The lane crosses the stream there. We could get ahead of the Judge."

But I can't see how we can make it. I realize now that a twig has scratched my face. I wipe my cheek and see my hand has streaks of red on it. Bella's face is marked too. She looks hot. I realize that she has the bag of provisions strapped to her back. I'm carrying nothing.

"Let me take that," I tell her. "My turn."

"Later," she says. "Not now. No time to lose."

She strides off and I follow her, crashing through the last of the trees, leaping the stream and across the field. We crawl through a gap in a hedge and begin sprinting along the lane, somehow immune to the possibility that we might be spotted. I am sure if I stopped running I would hear Butterworth's horse's hooves clattering up behind us.

We race over the bridge without looking back.

We move along a lane hidden by the high hedgerows on either side. Bella is running with her head down, not that this makes much difference, and I'm doing it too now. We keep running, the narrow lane winding like a silver stream in the glare of the day. The heat hammers down; my head begins to thump. Everything is beginning to drain of colour; the light is fierce, blinding.

Bella is slowing, I can hear the rhythm of the bag pounding against her back change. She is breathing heavily, walking. Shielding her eyes she looks ahead.

Looming up ahead is the colossal magnificence of Butterworth Tor. I realize now that it is far bigger than any of the other tors, and rises in stages until crowned by the white temple of palace that is Judge Butterworth's mansion.

And then a bugle call rips across from the tor.

Positioned halfway up, standing to attention before one of the numerous pristine outbuildings, ready to greet their great general, is a line of red-suited ash wardens, jostling into position, pulling at their jackets and setting their caps in place.

They have seen us. They have seen the Judge. They don't know whether to remain a guard of honour, or transform into a military field unit and give chase.

A bugle call from behind us gives a response. It is close, closer than either of us expected.

Bella doesn't hesitate. She grabs my hand and pulls me off the road and over a gate on to a piece of rough, sandy grass. We're running again and this time we seem to be heading for sand dunes.

"We'll stand out a mile here," she yells back at me. "But I don't think the Judge and his brigade will have the energy to follow us."

I don't reply. The Judge is on a horse. Didn't she notice?

The intense heat of the day seems to have been stored up in the dunes and is released the moment we set foot on them. I'm suddenly desperately thirsty. Our legs push on, every step seeming to require ten times the energy needed on the lane. It is brutally hot and each grain of sand dazzles and blinds us. The bugles sound again, and then, for the first time, I hear Butterworth.

"What in heaven's name are you doing?" he yells. I picture him in his ridiculous wig and his bright-red lips. I want to turn and scream back, "Escaping! What do you think?", but realize he's not shouting at us, he's shouting at his motley militia.

We emerge from the dunes on to a long strand of deserted white sand. After all this, will I end up leading Butterworth straight to Dad? Bella stops running for a moment and struggles to unstrap her bag. She holds it out for me. "Your turn," she says. It is far heavier than I supposed. No wonder she looks so hot. She glances along the beach then points towards Butterworth Tor. "I think we need to head that way. Follow the beach round the tor and find a way inland from there."

And then what? Can we go back to the stores and resume normal life? What will happen to us if we're caught? There's no more time to think. I pull on the bag, strap it up, then break into a canter behind Bella, who is already running again. We're heading into the shadow of Butterworth Tor.

In the corner of my eye I can feel the presence of the sun and the comet, still following each other around the sky. It's impossible to look directly up at them; the light is overwhelmingly bright. But something about the shape and colour of the light at the edge of my vision leaves me in no doubt, the comet is now the larger of the two. I can almost feel its vast spiralling tail, a violet blue smear, twisting around upon itself, a colour so intense it is not colour at all, just a sort of sinister radiance.

My eyes hurt, as if they are going to burst,

unable to bear the image of the comet imprinted upon them.

And the beach doesn't help. It is featureless and blank, a pulsating floor of light. Ahead of me, just about, I can see the black shimmer of Bella, almost a mirage, dissolving into the heat.

I keep running, although I don't sense I'm moving forward. There is no sound now, only the thump of my pulse in my head and the pounding of my feet on the ground. Light shimmers in pools and the dark hollows of distant caves become things in their own right. They come charging out at me, punching my head and my chest, dark bullets hammering at me, forcing me back, blow after blow, thump, thump.

This isn't my head. It's hooves. I swing round to see the horse and its squat jockey galloping across the sand from the dunes. He's alone, the red-suited wardens nowhere to be seen.

I don't know what to do. There's nowhere to run, the beach is too big, we're too far from any hiding place. With no alternative I stand and stare as the Judge, in a braided bright-green jacket, bounces on the saddle towards me.

The horse pulls up and shakes itself. Butterworth stares down hard, his face shiny, red and menacing.

"You, boy, you. . ." He's puffing heavily, still trying to catch his breath. Sweat pours down his forehead from the line of the wig, trickling into streams that cut through the cake of his make-up. He has his three-cornered hat pulled on top of the wig and strapped under his chin, keeping everything in place. He is wearing lipstick. It's smeared across his painted cheeks. The man is a dangerous clown. "The fortune-teller!" he says at last. "You can tell the future, can you? Well, predict what's going to happen now." He sneers and shakes his head. "You're coming with me," he says, "and we are going to get your wretched father!" He suddenly lurches forward and tries to grab me.

I hear a tearing sound. The Judge sits up, feels under his arm. His mouth contorts. He has ripped his jacket, and he blames me, obviously.

"Get up on the horse," he says. He expects to be obeyed.

I stare at him. I shake my head slowly at first.

"I said get up!"

My throat is dry. I don't want to speak; my voice will shake, I'll sound frightened. "No thanks," I say anyway. I begin to move backwards, stepping out of his reach.

He glares at me, kicks at the horse, which

begins to manoeuvre in a large circle around me. The horse looks a bit confused.

And now I can see Bella staring helplessly.

"Stay back!" I yell.

And then with another kick, and spray of sand, a sudden lunge, he has me with both hands and is pulling me up. I kick out, my heels hit the horse's belly and it swings round, unsure what is happening.

"You just sit. . ." I can smell him, the powdered wig, the gunk on his face, the sour stink of sweat and alcohol.

I kick again and this time the horse rears up. I feel us slipping and then we crash to the ground, my fall broken by the bag, the Judge crashing down on his back next to me. His hat has come off and so has his wig. He is utterly bald and now looks like a bloated boxer, flat out on the canvas, waiting for the count.

He opens his eyes, shields them from the glare, and looks around. "You . . . you. . ." The Judge's eyes bulge with rage.

I scramble to my feet. The horse stands over us, calmer now.

"I am going to make you suffer," he snarls, pushing himself up. I grab a handful of sand and throw it in his face. He yelps and covers his eyes.

Bella appears. She grabs the horse's reins. "Get on," she yells. "Get on."

I've never done this before, but I grab the saddle, put my foot in the stirrup, and scramble on. Then she's up too, behind me, and we're away.

I turn back to see the Judge on his knees. He looks as if he's been left stranded in the desert, and he's praying. Next to him is our bag; I've left it behind. Beyond him I see red-coated figures appear on the top of the dunes.

"Now we're really in trouble," Bella shouts over my shoulder.

I like it. I enjoyed filling his eyes with sand. I'm glad we've stolen his horse. But I have no idea what we're going to do next.

THiRTY-ONE

We begin rounding the headland, the sea still too far off to present any threat of cutting us off. The cliffs rise up menacingly, and the stretch of beach and the wide sweep of bay ahead seem even more desolate, more isolated and removed from the rest of the island.

"Look," says Bella, her face over my shoulder. "What's that?"

Where a second headland peters out into a string of rocks, in the shadow of the cliffs, are dark, crouching shapes. From here they look like insects, their mandibles working at the ground. One of the figures holds something up, a piece of cloth, or an empty sack, as some sort of signal to us. Bella urges the horse forward. It is remarkably compliant.

As we approach we see damp, half-filled sacks scattered around on the sand. The workers continue signalling to us, beckoning us forward.

Suddenly there's a semi-circle of them around

us. Old faces inspect us from the shadow of wide-brimmed rain hats. They wear shabby, oily clothes and rubber boots. One is smoking a clay pipe. They stare at us, their eyes narrowed against the light. All of them are wizened and small. There are no children, no one who looks younger than the oldest ash warden.

"Nice horse," says one nearest us, at last.

"Where d'you get that?" says another.

"Only one horse like that on the island," says a little old woman.

"And that belongs to the Judge!" says the man nearest us. And then he grins, and chuckles, and all the others chuckle too, like clucking hens, their shoulders shaking, their little toothless mouths pecking the air.

The old man at the front steps forward and sets his hand on the horse's neck. "If this is the Judge's horse, then unless you are his special friends, and you must be very special, 'cause no one is allowed to ride his horse, not ever, no. Unless you are his very, very special friends. . ."

"You've nicked the horse!" says the old woman, and they start again, shaking and clucking, their little eyes reduced to black crescents in their dark, wrinkled faces.

"You don't want to go far on that," says the old

man, "because if it ain't yours, and we don't think it is, then someone might just decide you need to be shot off it!"

They don't laugh any more.

"Are you sworn enemies of the Judge?" asks the old man.

Bella's voice comes from behind me. "Is this a good idea?" she whispers. "They probably want the horse themselves. For meat."

We are close to Butterworth Tor, and I sense we are being watched. The horse makes us easy to spot.

"Come on," I say to Bella, "let's get off." I drop down first, then she slides off slowly, far less comfortable with the idea.

"Now then," says the old man. "We don't want you following us around, do we?" And he slaps the horse so hard I can't believe it doesn't turn round and bite him. Instead it looks up, a little startled, and wanders off, towards the cliffs.

"Why don't we see if we can get you two back home," says the hooked-nose woman. "Before that nasty Judge catches up with you?" She holds up some old oilskins and a pair of mouldy rain hats. "You put these on. Keep your heads down. The Judge has the wardens out, looking everywhere. But they won't bother us. They leave us alone."

We follow them into a narrow cleft in the cliff. Narrow steps, so narrow rock brushes both my shoulders, take us up from the beach. Waiting at the top, munching the grass, is an old pony with a ramshackle cart fastened to it.

The old man signals to us to clamber up. The little hooked-nose woman sits next to us; the pipe smoker and the tiny old man sit opposite. A third takes the reins and gently orders their pony to begin the slow plod up a path between the cliffs and around Butterworth Tor.

"Now, dears," says the hooked-nose woman, "these are winkles, cockles and so on. Shellfish. We take this stuff to the market at Hook Head every day. Sometimes early, sometimes late. We don't seem to know any more!"

"Been doing it for hundreds of years," says the old man opposite us. He takes out a pipe and lights it.

"Well, not us, dears," says the old woman. "Generations. We go back hundreds of years."

We follow the rough track that runs around the edge of the Judge's vast estate.

"The Butterworths", says the pipe smoker, "took as much as they wanted. You see that?" He points the stem of his pipe towards a neat stone wall that follows the contour of the hill. "Ever wondered why he can grow such stuff, when just over the wall it's almost a desert?"

"The ash," says Bella. "Didn't he just buy all the good ash?"

"And took the rest," says the tiny one, almost spitting his words.

"Everyone is too afraid to fight back," says the old woman.

"But like the tides, fortunes come and go," says the pipe smoker again. He nods as he says this, as if it is something he was told when he was young and now he's seeing evidence of it himself.

"No, things don't look good for the Judge, do they?" says the hooked-nose woman. I don't understand. Things look very good for the Judge. He has all the ash he wants, and the wardens are his private army. "First he loses his horse, and now the Khoronos," she continues.

Bella has been silent for a while. But she shifts in her seat and leans forward. "What? The what?"

"The Khoronos," she says again. "That thing!" The old woman waves her thin arm in the direction of the light above her head.

"The comet?" I ask. "Is that what you call it? The Khoronos?"

"The Khoronos," she says. "This is its time, you know."

"Khoronos is our mother and father, our beginning and our end," says the pipe man, releasing a great cloud of smoke from his mouth. He sounds like Dad.

I get a tight, unpleasant feeling in my stomach. I feel Bella's hand on my arm.

"Don't you know anything, dears?" says the old woman. "You are from the Green and you don't know about the great Khoronos? No, I don't suppose. . ."

"It's a comet," I say again, trying to restore a little bit of science into the mumbo-jumbo.

"Call it what you like, dear," says the old woman, smiling.

"King Curlymane," says Bella, suddenly.

The winklers go quiet and look at each other. Then, without a signal, begin singing.

"King Curlymane has fire in his hair,
A nose that is frozen and a menacing glare,
Swings round the universe, disappears past the
sun,
King Curlymane has gold in his ears,
King Curlymane has gold in his ears,
He won't be back for five hundred years,
He won't be back for five hundred years."

"That was the song Dad taught me," shrieks Bella, "that was it, exactly!"

"King Curlymane is the comet?" I ask.

"I think these children need a little history lesson," says the tiny old man next to the pipe smoker. He's as wrinkled as the sea and probably as old. The little one stands, as if he's done this many times. "King Curlymane is just a song for children. We like to call the visitor by its more ancient name, Khoronos. Just as the earth wheels round the sun, so Khoronos turns in a great circle round the universe. It visits us just once every five hundred and eight years. When it comes, it brings destruction. It brings an end to things as they are."

"An end?" squeaks Bella. "What do you mean? The end of the world?"

The little old man steadies himself and considers this carefully. "Not the end of the world, my dears," he says, "just the end of things as they are."

"How do you know?" I ask, a little weary of all this mumbo-jumbo. "Who told you?"

He laughs at this. "Who told you the earth is round? Who told you about the planets and the stars?"

"I read about them!" I tell him. "I read about them in books!"

"Ah, but what if you couldn't read?"

"Then I wouldn't know!"

"Wouldn't you? Wouldn't you?"

"And this thing, the comet, Khoronos," says Bella, "it is a comet, is it?"

"It is nothing other than our fate, and our fortune!" the little man announces and folds his arms to indicate the lecture is over.

As we round Butterworth Tor some sense of normality returns when I see the Green below us, but it looks almost a dust bowl in the afternoon light. Ahead is the bleak rock of Blight's farm and, next to it, Clacker's sinister tor.

Blocking the junction with the island's only road, the lane that circles the island, is a line of red jackets: ash wardens. One of them steps forward and holds up his arm. He looks hot and squints up to the old man with the reins.

"Good afternoon, sir," says the ash warden, slightly impatiently. "Isn't this a little late to be heading for market?"

"Bad tides, this week," replies the man at the front. "We're at the mercy of the tides, you know."

The ash warden lifts his cap and scratches his head.

"We're looking for an escaped prisoner, one Jeremiah O'Connell. Tall, red-headed, bit of a beard. The Judge has been attacked by O'Connell's son, who stole his horse. Happened within the hour. Seen anything?"

The driver shakes his head. "Nothing to report, I'm afraid."

The warden shrugs and turns away. We trot past them, Bella and I keeping our faces hidden. When we're clear of the cordon I turn to see Bella looking at me. Her smile breaks into a laugh.

"You look ridiculous in that hat," she says. "How could anyone imagine you could be the destiny of Idlegreen?"

"I feel ridiculous too," I tell her. "And I'm about to cook."

Now that we're out of sight of the wardens I decide it's time to peel off the disguise. And time to say our goodbyes to the winkle pickers.

"Going somewhere?" asks the old woman as we throw down the oilskins.

"I have to get back to my mum," says Bella.

"Of course you do," says the old woman.

The pipe smoker yells something to the man at the reins and the cart comes to a halt.

"Thank you for helping us," says Bella, and she sounds sincere.

We're about to jump off the cart on to the bank

at the side of the lane when the pipe smoker says more: "You've seen the clocks, haven't you?"

Suddenly he has our attention again. Bella grips my arm. I nod. "Watch the thirteenth dial," he says, "because just about now it will be revealing the final phase."

"What does that mean?" I ask him, feeling a little angry as if we are being teased. Is he going to tell me I am the destiny of Idlegreen too?

"You must know the prophecy."

"The prophecy of the clocks?" asks Bella.

The little old man grins. "Yes," he says, "that's all part of it too." And his eyes close and he turns his face into the light.

"When he arrives upon the thirteenth dial,
on those who fortune has forsaken, now she smiles."

Exactly as Dryden Clacker said.

"Who arrives on the thirteenth dial?" asks Bella. "Who is it? Is it Oswald?"

The old man realizes Bella means me. He laughs. "You'll see, soon enough," he says. He looks away, grinning to himself. Bella and I drop into the grass, the old woman holds up an arm to signal her goodbye.

Clacker's Farm is just a stone's throw away and

I need some water. "I have to go up to Clacker's Farm," I tell Bella. "The comet, or whatever it is, there must be something about it in one of their books. And Dryden knows more than he's told us."

"I'll come with you," says Bella. "Mum can wait another hour. She won't be worrying yet."

And there's something else. I have to look at the clock. I want to see the thirteenth dial.

THIRTY-TWO

The farmyard is deserted. A few days of this heat have reduced it to a bleached, dusty wasteland. There is an eerie silence about the place, as if it has been abandoned.

We get to the farmhouse door and knock twice. The door is ajar.

"Mrs Clacker?" Bella calls.

No answer.

Bella puts her head around the door. "Mrs Clacker?" she shouts, her voice disappearing unanswered in the cool darkness of the old place. I squeeze past her, into the house and towards the clock. Bella follows me. The abrupt change of light, from the stark brilliance of the afternoon, to the gloomy passageway, makes it almost impossible to see anything.

But then the clock begins to emerge out of the shadow. My mouth is dry, and my stomach clenches. If there is something sinister about Idlegreen, I sense that at this moment it will be revealed to us. Together we lean forward and peer at the single blank face at the top of the clock, the thirteenth dial.

Bella cranes her head forward. Then, with a sigh of relief, she turns and looks at me. "It's just the same," she says. "Double nothing and the apostrophe. It's just the same."

A figure appears at the top of the stairs and looks down at us. "It is almost time," says Mrs Clacker, stepping into the passage and passing me. "Almost time for tea. Would you like some, Bella?" She puts an arm around Bella and leads her into the sitting room, towards an armchair.

"Mrs Clacker," I say, as calmly as possible. "Can I look at your books?"

Mrs Clacker plumps up a cushion for Bella, then looks up at me. "Yes, go on, Oswald, although I am surprised you need to know anything. You seem to know so much already. Wouldn't you rather just have a sit down? You look exhausted."

I can't help myself. I just blurt it out. "Khoronos," I speak the word as if it's a creature of the night, a man-eating beast that stalks the woods.

Mrs Clacker almost laughs. She is certainly smiling. She makes her way across the room towards the kitchen. "I know. I'll make a nice cup of tea."

"I need to use the library," I shout at her as she disappears. Bella turns and looks at me and indicates that I'm to get on with it.

I slip past the clock, suspicious of it. Pushing open the heavy door to the library I find the curtains drawn but a lamp is lit and several books lie open beside it on the table. I move past them, they don't seem to contain anything helpful.

I skirt the shelves, searching for some pattern, some sort of order to the books. There are dictionaries, and many huge leather volumes with bold black letters stamped on to rusty brown leather. There are at least ten of these, each embossed with the words *The Annals and Antiquaries of Idlegreen*. There are shelves of natural history, of birds and plants. There are large illustrated books of winding mechanisms, ploughs and wells.

I turn back to the books on the table. There are two volumes of *The Annals and Antiquaries of Idlegreen* open, one at the year 1788, the other at 1813. The print is tiny and is laid out in two narrow columns per page. There are no illustrations, nothing to guide or soothe the eyes. Just pages and pages of narrow columns of print.

But there are other books open out on the table. One is an atlas, or at least a collection of maps of the islands. There are names I recognize: All Sorrow, Many Winkles, Old Fang, Greater and Lesser Fury. There is no map of Idlegreen, no mention of it. I turn the pages rapidly, straining my eyes in the shimmering yellow light.

"I think this is what you are looking for," says a familiar monotonous voice from behind me. I turn to find Dryden Clacker, his eyes even more pale and watery than I remember them, his face haunted and sallow. His lip is swollen, as if he's been in a fight. His long index finger rests on a small book. "Although I don't suppose you'll have time to read it now."

Surprised by his sudden appearance I pick up the book and move round the table to the window.

"Don't open the curtains, please," he says. "The light will damage the books."

The title, in very ornate script, is:

A Measure of Idlegreene
by Thomas Kellow

The pages feel dry and crisp, as if they could, at any moment, crumble in my fingers. There are sketches, maps, and five or six paragraphs of difficult description. The language seems ancient.

I concentrate long enough to read two paragraphs.

The whole isle differeth very much from itselfe, by reason of the geographie: so that a man would marvelle to see the great alteration betwixte the lowlande and the high landes. In the deep vale of Idlegreene, shut in on all sides by a circle of loftie peakes, no more than five arrow shots in widthe, there lieth the remnants of the rock that was said to have fallen from the skye. The salt is said to be corrupt and is the work of the Devil, who cometh when the salt is spent. It may bring fortune and profit for some, but unless one taketh but a measure of Idlegreene salte, the Devil shall have his revenge.

"The Devil?" I can't help myself, I just yell it out and slam the book shut. "What is going on here? There's a comet falling out of the sky upon us, and you're telling me it is the work of the Devil? Don't any of your books just deal with facts, with truth?"

Dryden stares through me, unmoved. "It is the truth," he says. "You just can't understand it."

I shake my head in disbelief. This sounds just like Dad. Everyone sounds like Dad. He'll be bringing out the tea leaves next.

"You will see, Oswald," says Dryden. "Evil will come, men will become evil, men will become like devils." His swollen lip makes him look like a waxwork. "Mother will hurt me if she hears me tell you this. But I have to tell you the truth. You have seen the thirteenth dial, now, haven't you?"

"Yes. And?" I don't want to become part of his ridiculous magic.

"The clocks were designed for this moment, Oswald," he says, still sounding as if he is some sort of clairvoyant, the words coming from the spirit world. "Idlegreen has been waiting for this for five hundred years. Five hundred years." And then he closes his eyes.

And at that moment, from somewhere deep below us, or from above us, I can't tell, there is a deep vibration, a heavy resonance that quivers outside and inside of me all at once.

I push past him, shoving the book into his hands, and hurry out into the passage.

The clock's bell is so low I can feel it in my ribs. It is more of a vibration than a sound, and it is continuous, almost as regular as a heartbeat. I stand under the arch that connects the passage with the front room; the clock's deep tolling travels through the floor, the walls, too loud, far too loud for just marking the hour.

Mrs Clacker appears with a tray. "I hope Dryden is keeping his mouth shut," she says, smiling menacingly. "He is so desperate to tell you our little secrets. But I suppose it doesn't matter now." And despite standing there, holding the steaming pot, she has her eyes closed.

I look across at Bella. "The clock, has it done this before?"

But I know the answer by the look on her face.

And I turn and find the thirteenth dial. Something is happening to it.

"Bella!" I yell. I don't hear her approach me but she's suddenly there, next to me. "Bella, it's changing!"

It's suddenly clear. For five hundred years the thirteenth dial has shown nothing but the strange two circles and the apostrophe. But now it comes alive. It looks harmless enough here, but there is absolutely no doubt about what it means.

As the clock's bell continues to chime I can detect a faint whirring from behind the dial. First a tiny green dot is revealed on the first circle. Then, the apostrophe shifts its angle slightly on to the larger, second circle and, as it does so, it changes colour. It becomes a tiny gold, purple and green feather, a wispy comma. It's the comet.

And now it has settled into place on the final

stage of its journey. The large "O" is the orbit of the comet, the smaller "O" the orbit of the earth. And where they touch is the point of catastrophe, the collision.

Bella is still holding her face and has turned away from the clock to look back into the sitting room. The chime is a chilling portent of doom. I want it to stop. I want to take a hammer to the clock and smash it, just for upsetting Bella.

Mrs Clacker, still standing where she was when the chimes began, opens her eyes. "The last hours," she says. "It will come during the night."

"Tonight?" I can't help crying out. "Tonight?"

Dryden Clacker appears at the other end of the passageway.

"Soon it will be the hour of Khoronos," he announces. "Prepare yourself for the darkness that is to come."

THiRTY-THREE

I grab Bella's hand and head for the door. We race across the farmyard, a cloud of dust rising behind us. The light is fierce, bleaching the landscape into a harsh and unfamiliar world.

We crash down the tor, vaulting a gate and a stile and leaping through a hedge to cut off a corner. When we reach the edge of the Green it's immediately obvious something is happening. People are spilling out of their cottages; some are running, others are walking, stunned and unsure. One man is lurching across the lane with a sandwich in his hand.

A woman stumbles from her home cradling a baby. An elderly couple hobble from their cottage. From inside I can hear the hard, cold chimes of a clock.

Bella rushes ahead of me, towards the stores. Her mother spots us through a window. Bella flies towards Elizabeth, leaping up to hug her. I'm left standing there, looking at my feet, away from the light.

"Bella," I hear her mother whisper, smoothing her hair. "What's happening?"

"The clocks, Mum," she says, still trying to catch her breath. "They have revealed the thirteenth dial, and the chimes, the chimes are so horrible."

I look back at them now. Elizabeth is staring at me, Bella is explaining what we have just seen on the dial.

Perhaps this is the end of the world. I can't believe Dad was right all along.

And, of course, I wish so much that he could appear now, with that insane grin, announcing he has found some miraculous way of getting off the island.

"What do we do?" I hear Bella squeal into her mother's arm. "What do we do?"

But there isn't anything we can do.

I shield my eyes and watch as twenty or so villagers gather together on the Green. Beyond, on Butterworth Tor, I make out a line of red-suited wardens. Following the island across, towards Morden Tor, I spot another group of them; these are sitting, watching events unfold as if this was all a cataclysmic entertainment.

The Judge is nowhere to be seen. Perhaps he

knows his reign of terror is nothing compared to this thing that hangs over us.

"It can't be the end of the world," sobs Bella. "It can't be, it's not fair."

And then, for the first time I feel scared.

On the faces of the villagers on the Green I watch as confusion becomes dread. People run from their houses on to the Green; others are running away. A family hurry past us, their eyes glazed, their faces ghostly white. They rush on, heading for the path that takes them up Mill Tor.

Two young children are being chased by their mother. They think it's a game, they are giggling and screeching with delight. Their mother runs after one, then the other, an arm outstretched, calling after them. She is sobbing uncontrollably and now and again turns to look at the comet.

Then Dusty appears. He is wheeling his bicycle along the lane. He sees the commotion on the Green, then looks up at the corona of light. He drops his bike and falls to his knees.

We watch as the sun drops behind Blight's Tor leaving King Curlymane alone above us, magnificent in its grotesque and terrifying beauty.

The panic ceases. There is an abrupt stillness. Everyone is spellbound.

The comet is a huge swirl of green and purple,

and it fills the dome of the sky. Its head is a sinister black point and from this bursts a huge spray of light, like fine coloured hair, winding around itself. A vast silver halo surrounds it, King Curlymane's crown.

We are its servants now, and we must submit to it. There is no more we can do. We walk towards the others on the Green, and as we approach, they greet us solemnly with extended arms.

It's as if we've joined a new society.

Bella and Elizabeth know them all, of course. They hug each other and look into each other's eyes with sorrow and acceptance. Diana and Miranda are there, holding hands, staring upwards, hypnotized.

Something whistles through the air above us, a high-pitched siren, something spinning and falling to earth. Then it happens again.

We look around, at each other, at the sky whisked and whorled above Blight's Tor.

There is a sudden burst of missiles, four, five, six, it's hard to keep count. They sizzle through the air, unzipping the sky above our heads, but its impossible to know where they land. Then one hits the Green, just behind us, sending up an eerie column of dust.

An old man gasps, a woman screams.

Another one hits the Green, closer this time, punching a small crater in the ground and sending out a shower of soil and small stones.

Then there's a sound like steam being released from a boiler and, careening over us, we gape at a fireball, perhaps no bigger than a fist. It's white hot and it leaves a trail of light after it that at first is a brilliant arc, but soon slowly fades into evening sky.

Now the sun has completely gone and the swirl of the comet's tail dominates the western sky. The evening is suddenly full of crackles and tiny explosions. A second bombardment of the Green begins, but this time it doesn't relent. Bella and I watch in stupefied amazement as a shower of fizzing meteorites crackles down around us. The ground thumps and hisses, the soil spits and puffs, and shards and rocks begin spinning off in every direction.

We hear the trees at the edge of the Green take hit after hit and then the air is alight, bursting with sparks, which paint spirals and twists of light. From somewhere behind the cottages on the lane we hear a crash and a dog starts barking, then howling.

I realize then that we are entering the life of the thing itself; the gases surrounding the earth and the plume of the comet are forging a new, alien sky.

The heavens light up now, cascading with golds and greens and purples and blues, a cacophony of cracks and whistles and deep, echoing booms.

"We have to get out of here," Elizabeth shouts suddenly. "Get under cover, come on, run! Run!" I'm so overawed by the spectacle I can't break away from it. It's happening, it's happening all right. Bella grabs me and tries to pull me away from the Green, but I'm staggering, losing my balance. I want to watch the world end but I'm being dragged away towards the safety of the stores.

When we get inside Elizabeth slams the door and locks it. Almost immediately there is a thunderous crash and we hear something collapse but don't know if it's next door, or further away. There are screams and the sounds of feet running. We gather behind the counter and push up against the window to look out, Elizabeth muttering how silly we are, that if the window shatters we'll all be cut to pieces.

But the world outside is not one we recognize, it looks like the surface of a distant star. The sky looks poisoned now, heavy with deep blue-grey swirls and streaks of acrid yellow. And black rocks are falling, the size of lumps of coal. They smash down on to the lane, shattering into shrapnel.

They rain down upon the roof, an intense, deafening assault. It's as if we are inside the comet now, right inside it, wrapped up in its tail, with its monstrous black eye circling the earth, toying with us, squeezing around us.

We move away from the window, reaching out like the blind for the comfort of a wall, or a solid surface. I follow Bella, who is trailing after her mother into the storeroom and then into the kitchen. There are no windows here. The sound is not so terrifying.

Bizarrely, Elizabeth pulls out a chair and sits at the table, dropping her face into her hands. Bella pulls a stool next to her; she sits close and hugs her. I stand against the stove, looking up, waiting for the moment the roof is torn away, or the whole house is lifted up, and us with it.

For a few moments I'm absorbed in imagining how the end will come, excited by it. I want to see something and hold on to it for as long as I can. And if I'm propelled into the air, I want to be awake and aware, I want to enjoy it. Why not? Why shouldn't I?

It is about to happen. We can't just pass through this now, the comet must hit, and now that we are inside it, now that it envelops us I have to accept all the stories, all the nonsense had some truth. This is Dad's catastrophe, just as he wanted it. I find that I'm laughing, head right back, hysterical, laughing at the way he spelt it. I see his gawky letters before my eyes.

CATASTROFE

And all I can hear is screaming; screams as the roof crashes in. Screaming as the world ends, as everything folds in on itself, collapses and dies.

THIRTY-FOUR

I don't think dead is like this. Dead is dead. This is not it. This may be some other place, but I'm not dead.

There is no sound, other than someone's breathing, probably my own. There is darkness, utter darkness, like I've never seen before. And there is thick, choking dust, the dust of outer space.

I'm not floating, I'm on the ground.

Yes, I'm on the earth. I can smell it. I can taste it too; my mouth is full of it. Dust, debris, splinters of wood, shards of tiles and rough, scratching grit, brick dust, perhaps. I'm covered with the stuff. I try and sit up but there's no room.

The silence is confusing. There are no screams, there is no terror. Yet something has happened, something terrible. I move one leg, then the other and begin a slow, careful crawl. First there's a cupboard, then a wall, and a door. Then I find an opening. Again, I try to stand but there's an obstruction. I stick to crawling, my mouth filling with more dust. Thick dust and earth and just enough air but no light.

Something of the last few moments before the devastation comes into my head. Bella, Elizabeth, at the table. But I don't know where anything is now. Everything has been smashed, crushed and rearranged. No point in trying to work out where they are.

Another doorway and the air tastes colder, clearer. Yes, I'm under the hatch of the stores, I know where I am. And the door to the outside must be. . .

Something is not right. It is obvious but I don't want to admit it to myself. I look up. The store extends upwards, almost infinitely into the darkness. The roof has gone. Above me is night, thick, filthy night.

And now I'm standing in the doorway, and the door has gone too. And somewhere out there is the Green. I am stepping into a fog, a cloud of swirling particles, something like soot, and there are flakes of grey stuff, hanging there, dropping all around.

Perhaps I am the only survivor, there's just me left to wander for ever through the grimy atmosphere of a new, ugly world.

I'm in the lane. I turn to look back but there's nothing much to see. The walls of the stores, the windows don't seem too damaged. Except all the glass from the windows has gone.

And then I see something on the Green. At first I think it's the kinks and blurs of my light-damaged eyes. But it isn't. Out there in the night, scattered over the Green, are gleams and glows of hot embers, little red spots that flicker and die as I watch. Pieces of the comet, hundreds of pieces lie scattered over the island. I can see a thick band now, a giant graze, a long ribbon of burning rock, glowing through the dust, trailing over the Green towards the sand dunes. I step through the gap in the wall, careful where I tread. I'm unsteady enough, and having survived the catastrophe, I don't want to trip and land face down in red-hot rock.

I don't have to go far until I reach the first piece. Squatting down, I see it's no bigger than an apple. But it seems to glow from the inside and creates a globe of brightness. It illuminates the tiny, thick, lush blades of grass that push up around it, cradling the rock there, tenderly, like the flat fingers of a microscopic creature buried in the soil.

I push myself up into a standing position; hold

myself steady, just to make sure I'm not going to suddenly topple over. There are some larger, bright rocks further ahead. I want a closer look. I step carefully, still half dazed.

The glow from these larger specimens is almost beautiful. Some of them have a white core and are like orange fruit, others are almost pink. They shimmer and pulsate. Like discarded lamps, they light up great circles of delicate new grass. The larger rocks remind me of shrines, the places I've seen on the other islands dedicated to fisherman lost at sea. They are garlanded with wreaths of the dense new grass. The grass looks as if it has just sprung out of the soil and seems to be growing even as I stare at it.

It is.

And then I realize what I'm looking at. And as soon as I realize it my eyes fill with tears. In an instant the entire history of the island snaps into place, like a jigsaw assembling itself before my eyes.

I turn and run as fast as I can, back towards the stores. Because knowing what I know now, they must have survived. They have to survive. It doesn't make any sense if they haven't, it just doesn't make any sense.

The dust inside the stores repels me at first,

then I hold my hand over my face and charge in, diving blindly under the counter and through to the kitchen.

"Bella!" I call. "Bella, Elizabeth!"

There's no reply, nothing. I feel in front of me. I find the table, the chairs. One of them is damaged, a large splinter of wood sticking out at an odd angle.

They're not in here.

I try to imagine I'm them, work out their movements. I crawl under the table and forwards, through to the hallway, here too the air is thick with choking soot and plaster. There's the turning into the stairway. I follow it, still imagining I'm them, perhaps disoriented; they don't know where they are.

And what if I can't find them? Or worse, what if I find them, and they haven't survived? I steel myself for the worst, then push any further thoughts away and move up the stairs. I find myself outside Bella's bedroom door. I go to knock but the door isn't there. I don't want to call out again, just in case there's no answer. But I have to.

"Bella?" I call into the emptiness. "Bella, are you. . ."

And then I hear breathing, just a little, but I know then someone else is alive.

I step in. "Bella?" I reach out a hand. I find the pillow, the bed; she's not there.

"Here," she whispers. "Oswald?"

I reach under the bed and touch her face. "Bella?"

"Oswald?" It's her.

"Bella, where's your mother? Where's Elizabeth?"

"Here," says another voice. They are both lying there, under the bed.

"Are you all right?"

And at that moment there's a crash above us. Something hits the roof and tumbles down. We listen as a few smaller rocks seem to follow, and then there's silence again.

"Oswald," says Bella. "We thought you were dead."

"Never mind, I'm not. Not yet. Are you all right?" I realize I've asked this already.

"Get under here," says Elizabeth. "We need to stay here until morning. Until we know it's safe. It's not over yet."

"The roof of the shop has gone," I blurt out and immediately wish I hadn't.

I hear Elizabeth whisper something to herself.

"And this roof could go next," says Bella, "get under here."

I slide under the bed, next to them. I feel one blanket, then another, pushed over me. I want to tell them about the Green, I want to tell them now but I also want to keep it until morning. But, after the terror of the day, in a few seconds, I'm asleep.

THiRTY-fiVE

The sounds that surround me and the sounds in my head, it's hard to separate what's real from what isn't. Thunderous chimes resonate in my skull, low vibrations rising from the earth's core. Nightmare and reality merge, then slip apart. A flood of colour rushes in and churns around my head; there are flashes and arcs of white fire.

Clouds burst with stars, but reaching up to touch them I disturb Bella and my knuckles hit the underside of the bed. The clouds form globes of gold and orange, white and alive at the core, scintillating eyes.

The eyes swivel to look at me, hundreds of them. The ground shakes, rumbles, the eyes bounce about, like rocks in a sieve. The sound is too real to be a dream. The eyes sprout lashes, curling lashes of green.

The tufts of new grass, I imagine them on Dad's face, like the growth of his beard. I see him dancing, grinning, the man on the Green; he's the green man. The world has come to an end. The green man is dancing over the smoking ruins, skipping off, over the sea, leaving me behind.

It should be morning, but it isn't. I know it should be morning by now. It's still too dark. My nightmare is dissolving, I'm surfacing back into the waking world.

Bella is elbowing me. "I think we should take a look around," she says. "I'm prepared for a shock."

"Have you been awake for long?" I ask her.

"Don't know. My lungs feel like they're on fire."

I want to tell her what I saw last night but I'm not certain what has happened and what hasn't. My memory is muddled. I try and picture the Green as I think I saw it, with the rock lamps, but I keep seeing the green man, Dad sprouting with grass, dancing a jig, stepping between the burning rocks.

"I've been awake for ages," she says. "I've heard nothing for a while. I think I heard the earth quake in the night, heard it, didn't feel it."

"Yes," I know what she means, "the ground was rumbling, I remember. But I thought I was dreaming." I don't know what I dreamed and what I saw.

Elizabeth is still snoring loudly but Bella shakes her. "Mum. It's stopped," I hear Bella whisper.

Elizabeth stirs and then tries to sit up but hits her head on the underside of the mattress.

The three of us slide out from beneath the bed and struggle to our feet. The darkness is a little strange. It isn't the darkness of night, more the darkness of winter, of a late afternoon in December.

But it's a summer's morning.

"Dust, I expect," says Elizabeth, moving to the window. "Dust left in the air from last night."

We make our way downstairs and straight outside, still in the clothes we dressed in yesterday morning. It's been a very long twenty-four hours. Elizabeth makes no sound as we pass through the stores. She looks up, gives a little shake of the head and follows me to the door.

In the lane the sky is thick with soot, heavy with particles and flakes that jump about on wispy eddies of air. The sky seems to have no beginning, or at least it begins where the ground ends. Everywhere is grey. There are swirling clouds and buffeting currents. Nothing too hostile or threatening, nothing except thick comet dust.

Scanning the Green I realize whatever was burning here last night is now snuffed out. But the disappearance of the glow doesn't concern me. It wasn't that I wanted to show them.

"You did say, didn't you, that the Green was your land?" I ask, just to make sure.

"It's ours," replies Elizabeth, "for what it's worth." She turns to look at the stores. "We don't have much else now."

"I think you might," I say, pointing out to the Green. I should contain myself, until I can be sure. "Come and see this." I can't help it now, I'm grinning. They're confused. What can be out on the Green that can compensate for the loss of their home?

Bella and Elizabeth take in what I haven't noticed yet. Many of the cottages close to the stores have been hit. All that remains of one house is a mound of rubble.

"Poor woman," sighs Elizabeth. "Poor Miss Hobbes. Look at her place!"

I can't keep quiet for much longer. Elizabeth is snivelling, standing stone-cold still in the middle of the lane with her daughter's arm around her. At last Bella releases her grip and walks towards me. Elizabeth, still holding her face, turns.

"Come and look," I say, trying to keep composed. I want to shout at them, I want to jump up and down and yell at them. But I don't.

"Look at it!" cries Bella, when she sees the Green. "Heavens above, look at it!"

The Green is pocked with craters. Most are no bigger than a dinner plate but here and there are larger ones, one or two big enough to climb into.

"Come on, wait until you see. . ." I march on, ahead of them, looking for what I saw last night. I picture them in my head, the burning coals, the orange-red embers.

But there's something that disturbs me. There are tracks through the layers of the dust and soot, tracks of a horse and cart, criss-crossing each other.

And then I see the sprouts of green. "Look," I shout, they're still a way behind. "Look at the grass. Look at all this, all this new growth!" There's no doubting it now. I am certain, absolutely certain what I saw was real. "You know what this is, don't you? This comet dust, the comet that passes across us every five hundred years? Do you see what it brings?" I feel like some sort of hysterical prophet, I'm trying not to let myself whirl out of control. I can feel so much of Dad in my voice. "It's rained down all over your property. It's all yours! The comet dust, it's yours!"

"What?" says Elizabeth, confused and tearful. The look on her face suggests she thinks I'm losing my mind.

Bella's eyes widen, her jaw drops. She stares at

the clumps of fresh grass. "Ash," she says at last. "Idlegreen ash!"

"Yes! Yes!" I holler, laughing. "It's how it came before, and it has come again and. . ."

"But, Oswald," says Bella. "Where is it?"

I don't know what she means. I look around, trying to point it out to her. I can see the tufts of growth, everywhere, circles of grass of different sizes, hoops and quoits and wedding rings, even tiny shoots of plants that have been triggered by the fall.

But the large lumps of the stuff, the stuff I saw last night, still burning. It's all gone.

There are a few tiny rocks, here and there. But there were cartloads of it here last night.

Cartloads.

I whip around to look up at Butterworth Tor. It doesn't seem possible. I can't believe that he could do something so blatantly, in full view of everyone. But he has. I know he has.

"Bella," I gasp out. "We heard the wheels rumbling in our sleep."

"He's been here during the night," I tell them, "Butterworth! Butterworth and his gang of ash wardens. They've taken the lot. They've stolen it all. Stolen it!" I can hear my own voice rasping and screaming.

Bella and Elizabeth stand together, looking at the evidence.

"Perhaps you were mistaken, Oswald," says Elizabeth.

"But what about the grass, look, here, and here." I dance about, kicking at the bright grass, at the sprouts and shoots. I can tell Elizabeth doesn't want to see. She doesn't want to know.

There are voices coming from the lane, next to the stores. A small crowd is gathering. They look like they are consoling each other; arms reach out to support an old woman who seems unable to stand.

"It's Miss Hobbes," says Elizabeth. "Thank goodness she is all right. Poor thing, I must help her." Without another word Elizabeth rushes off towards them, a trail of dust following her.

"We need proof," I mutter, following the tracks, trying to see some pattern in them.

"It won't count," says Bella dismissively. "He can take what he likes, he can do exactly as he pleases. There's no law here except his."

"And Blight's helped himself too," I add. "Look!"

Several sets of tracks lead off the Green towards Butterworth Tor, but there are a few that head towards Blight Tor.

"We need to get up there, see for ourselves," I

tell her. "We have to do something. This ash, it's yours. It belongs to the stores, to you and Elizabeth."

"Even if it is what you think it is," says Bella, "it's not ours any more." And she turns away and starts walking towards her mother.

I run after her and catch up. "So what are you going to do now? What is left for you? What else is there left to do but to fight back?"

Bella doesn't reply. She keeps walking, her eyes focused on the little group outside the stores.

"Bella, the ash that landed on the Green is yours. Think of what you could do with it. You would be able to grow all that you could ever need, and there would be so much left, pots and pots of it. . ."

I can't believe this is happening. Butterworth has beaten us before we could even begin.

I stop walking and watch Bella exit through the gap in the wall, joining the women in the lane.

I'm getting cold now. It's still early morning but the sky, if anything, is getting darker. A huge trail of ash and soot still hangs in the air. To the south, over the dunes, I can just make out a thin strip of blue sky. I look directly up.

Flakes spiral and bob, a sinister black snow.

And I imagine all the dead butterflies in the

City Museum, released by a sudden cataclysm from their shattered glass cases. I see the poor creatures blown upwards by a wind that wants to torment them, mimicking the freedom of flight they once had. It's like it is now.

The sky is full of ash butterflies.

I kick at the ground and the feeble layer of ash, and the old soil beneath that.

And what was it the book in the Clackers' library said? The Devil's revenge. Evil will have its way. The good get nothing.

I'm not going to let things end like this.

THiRTY-SiX

Bella and Elizabeth begin by taking anything that can be salvaged into the storeroom. First I pull out the beams that have collapsed; there aren't many. Then I move the fallen slates, stacked like the pages of book, out into the garden at the back, and place them in neat piles along the inside of a low brick wall. I move quietly, avoiding any conversation. There's nothing much to say now. Everything looks hopeless.

This has been a catastrophe, after all. My father, despite his lunatic ways, has been right all along.

Why should I have imagined that I knew everything? I have this faith, this trust in the truth, in the right way to do things, in using my eyes and ears to decide what I know. Dad's crazy beliefs will always be a mystery to me.

Look at the island, look how lives are ruined by a crook who calls himself a judge, a man who can help himself to whatever he wants. It now seems obvious to me that there is no justice in the world, that things don't work the way they should. There is no right and wrong, just the way things are.

When I drop the slates I'm dropping them on Butterworth's head. I see his red cheeks and his plump lips, I see the powder rising from his wig. And for a second I can laugh at the memory of him left sprawling on the beach, as Bella and I disappear on his horse.

So much has happened since then.

After an hour or so of shifting slates I begin sweeping. There's a heaviness to the air. Even sound feels trapped and muffled. Nothing echoes as it should, stone doesn't sound like stone. I know my voice would sound hollow if I spoke; it would sound weak and mean.

I drop the broom on to the floor. It's so gloomy in here I don't want to continue. I think about going to the others, talking to them. But I have nothing to say. I slip behind the counter, which has survived unscathed from the collapse, and pull out the tall stool.

Automatically my hands search out the ledger and the ink. I open the book and feel some satisfaction when it falls open at the right page. I dip the pen and, almost in a trance, completely without any idea of what I am doing, at the top of a new, blank page, I begin to write.

by Oswald Smith, of Idlegreen Stores, 5,000
pots of best ash

And immediately I stop, horrified. I'm doodling on the ledger, a record of the shop's sales going back twenty years, maybe more. My doodle, my empty-headed scribble, is an admission that the life of the stores has come to an end. If Bella and Elizabeth see what I have done they will hate me. It looks callous and stupid.

I check to see if they are around and, when I'm convinced I'm alone, I very carefully begin removing the defaced page.

It's easier than I imagine; it comes away neatly and doesn't leave a trace. And because the book is bound in sections, I'm able to remove its loosened partner a few pages on without leaving any clues to what I've done.

Immediately I close the ledger and push it under the counter.

I punch the cash button on the till and the drawer crashes open. I push it back until it clicks, then prod the button again. It's a good feeling. I'm punching Butterworth's nose and the cash drawer is his bottom jaw, filled with gold and silver teeth, flying open as I hit him. I slam the drawer back into place, then punch my finger in his eye.

A ten-shilling note lying in the drawer of the till suggests something to me, something vague and impossible. I pull out the note and study it. "Butterworth's Bank", it says across the top. There's a portrait of the Judge and a delicate etching of Idlegreen. The spider insignia sits on a web of patterned loops and flourishes.

And now I have an idea. Just the germ of an idea and it won't go away. It gets more ridiculous the more I think about it. But as there is nothing else to do, I begin.

I have two big sheets of thick, old paper, a pot of black ink and a pen. With these mighty weapons I will bring Judge Butterworth to his knees.

THIRTY-SEVEN

I'm still working an hour later, when Bella, stepping softly through the storeroom, brings me a big mug of tea and a plate of ginger cake.

"It's expensive stuff," she says, "you better enjoy it."

Surprised by her sudden appearance I try to hide my work. But I'm not quick enough. She drags one piece of paper across the counter towards her and stares at it. She looks up at me, then back to the paper. "What is this all about?" she asks. She doesn't seem to notice, or care, that the pages are torn from the ledger. She picks up the sheet and holds it in front of her. The light in the stores is poor and she wants to study my efforts using the lamplight seeping out from the kitchen. "What are they, Oswald?"

"Just doodles, something to keep me amused," I tell her. I slurp the tea and break off a piece of the ginger cake. "Do we have to do the clocks this afternoon?"

Bella sighs. "I don't know how many are left. I think, under the circumstances, we can be excused." She lifts the counter and wanders into the ash-layered floor of the stores. It's just a shell now, and very depressing. "When you've eaten I think we should go and explore," she says. "Go and see who's been hit and who's survived."

"I want to go up to Butterworth's," I mumble through a mouthful of crumbs. "See where he's put all your ash."

Bella gives me a strange look, as if I'm unable to accept the truth of what has happened to her and her mum. Then her mood brightens a little and she shrugs. "What have we got to lose?" she says.

"Well, he could throw us off the cliff," I say with a grin. "Or get us to dress up in silly clothes."

Bella disappears for a few moments and returns wearing her long black coat, buttoned to the neck. It looks military and far too heavy and thick for a summer's day. But it isn't summer here, it's a grim, new season, one that feels like it will last for ever. A louring season of perpetual twilight.

"Did you say anything to your mum?"

"I told her we're going for a walk."

I grab my sheet of doodles and stuff them into the till.

Bella fills two baskets with food that will go to

waste in the devastated shop. "You never know," she says as we step out into the lane.

It must be early afternoon now and the sky is darker and heavier. The thick, ash-filled air stirs menacingly above the Green.

"Look at it," she says, heading for the gap in the stone wall. "Sunless noon."

Even from here I can see ash wardens busy on Butterworth Tor. Two, or maybe three carts are parked outside a long shed. Further down I can see Butterworth himself, moving along a row of workers.

"They're digging in the ash," I tell Bella, "look, it's obvious. That's your stuff, all of it."

"Forget it, Oswald," she says. "Butterworth is a crook and Blight is even worse. He slides around behind Butterworth, taking what the big man leaves in his wake."

"Like a hyena," I add. Up on Blight Tor there's no sign of any activity. If he has helped himself to ash, and I'm sure he has, then he's lying low. Blight doesn't have the Judge's firm belief that anything on Idlegreen is his. Blight knows he's a thief.

As we cross the Green I try to explain to Bella my plan to get back at Butterworth. She listens in silence, nodding her head.

"So we're going to fight him with paper money,

are we?" she says eventually. She doesn't seem very impressed and we continue walking in silence, staring up at Butterworth Tor, daring him, or his henchmen, to come and get us.

But they are not interested now, they have better things to do.

And as we cross the Green so the day gets darker and the thick blanket of cloud above us gets lower and heavier and seems to sag under the weight of all the debris the comet has left in its wake. The comet has not hit the earth. Its tail has been dragged across the planet's surface, bombarding the oceans and maybe other islands with debris, leaving a trail of ash and a scar of devastation.

The lane is strewn with fragments and layered with a mixture of ash, soot and comet dust. The tracks of Butterworth's wagons sweep between two open gates and up through his estate, running between an avenue of tall Scots pines. Terraces of lawns lie either side of this drive and then, further to the left, beyond a line of a long, well-tended garden hedge, the plantations begin. It's here that the wardens and other workers move around the carts, unloading, raking and mopping brows.

The gloom of the afternoon and the grim,

collapsing sky make everything seem spent, used up and finished.

Bella and I saunter through the gates, each of us swinging a basket of the store's best produce, as if we're about to go for a picnic. I am excited by the thrill of a confrontation with the Judge, and terrified too. A tiny stream tumbles through an ornamental garden, bouncing down a carefully cut path that ends in a splashing pool.

"Look," says Bella, "he's even got a wishing well."

I reach under the hedge to find a stone and, after pausing to take aim, lob it into the well. There is a soft, satisfying plop and I make my wish. "For swift and sweet revenge."

Bella nudges me gently on, along the hedge, until it curves round at the top of the rock garden. We are now in full view of Butterworth's vast home. The fine layer of dust on its roof and the spinning flakes of ash that fall between it and us, give it a macabre, sinister appearance.

The gravel drive splits into two here and runs either side of the house. But it also circles around and rejoins itself, allowing, I imagine, a coach to draw up to the front door, so that the pompous dandy can waddle up the steps without exerting himself too much. Knowing the drive on the far side of the house leads to a cul-de-sac I urge Bella to take the opposite route.

The circular drive has a neat lawn within it. This lies below the centre of the house and is laid with intricate patterns of flowers and sculpted shrubs. Nothing moves, there are no birds, not even an insect.

There are no butterflies, except the butterflies of dead ash.

It reminds me of a doll's house and, like a doll's house, it looks empty of warmth and life.

Bella walks with a strut, as if she wants to be seen. I'm not sure if it's such a good idea, but I try and copy her swagger. "Butterworth!" she yells suddenly. "How do you manage to fit into such a small house!"

The mansion stares back at us, the windows reflecting the grim weight of the afternoon. Suddenly a side door opens and a woman appears. She's wearing an apron and looks flushed.

"What do you want?" she shouts.

We wander towards her as if we're just passing through.

"Good afternoon," I say, as politely as I can. "We were wondering if you needed any food. We're a sort of charity, you see. We give donations to the needy."

The woman stares at me. She doesn't see the joke.

I can see Bella masking her grin with a hand.

We amble over to the woman and I put my basket down in front of her. I gesture to Bella to do the same.

"We've got tinned meats, fruit, some delicious bread. What would you like?"

The woman's face lights up. "Well, I'm just one of the cooks here," she says, "but, well, if it's free, then, can I . . . can I take it all?"

"You want both baskets?" I ask, smiling indulgently. I look at Bella. "Do we allow someone to have two baskets?"

Bella looks stunned but then says, "Only . . . the most needy."

"Ah yes," I continue, "that's right. Only the most needy. Are you the most desperate of all people in these parts? Have you suffered badly from the recent devastation? We're new around here, just arrived, difficult to tell the haves from the have-nots."

"Could we look inside the house," says Bella, "just to check?"

"Oh no, I couldn't let you come in," says the cook. "It's not for me to. . ."

"Well, we would only want to peep," I tell her.

"Just a little look, and then we'd leave you all this. For yourself, or your family."

The cook disappears inside for a few seconds, perhaps checking if the coast is clear. "Well, if you can be very quick."

We follow her in, passing through what I presume is a scullery, and then a storage area until we come into a big kitchen. The ceiling is high and beamed. Along one wall is a huge stove, big enough to sleep on. Next to this, arranged carefully, and ready for the knife, are three, or maybe four hares, their fur glistening. Pots and pans hang from the wall and on the opposite side of the room there is a huge dresser laden with crockery. I can see through a door to a pantry in which the shelves are straining under the weight of meats and cheese and bread.

Bella takes my basket from me and places both on the large table in the centre of the kitchen. "Would you like to examine the produce?" she says to the woman. But she already has her fat arms in one of them and is pulling out a loaf of bread and a jar of jam.

"These look very nice," she says.

I take this opportunity to slip past her and through a door in the far corner of the room. There's a short passageway that leads to a grand hallway. A wide staircase sweeps down towards the main doors.

At the far end of the hall, below a giant stag's head mounted on a colossal plinth, is something I hadn't expected to find here. But now I see it, I realize how much Judge Butterworth knew about the return of the comet.

It looks quite modest, standing below the powerful head of the stag. It's one of the clocks.

Turning, I hurry back to the kitchen, to find the cook placing the last of the things on the table.

"Yes," she says, "I'll take them all."

"Just one thing," I say, and as she looks up it's obvious she hasn't noticed my temporary disappearance. "The night the comet fell, did the clock here chime in a way it never has before?"

Bella flinches, as if she's been stung. Her face drains of colour. She looks at me and mouths the word "clock?".

"Oh yes," says the cook, replying to my question. "Made a terrible noise. And the Judge, he had everyone up all night, ready. He had so many preparations. Well, they were working flat out to gather in the stuff, you know. And what a harvest it was, what a harvest. All that beautiful ash. So clever of the Judge to know about these things. Well, that's why he lives in a place like this. He was out all night collecting up the stuff." She pauses for a second. "How did you know about the clock?"

"I thought everyone on the island had one," I reply.

"We have to be going now," Bella says suddenly and begins putting things back in the baskets. "We've heard enough."

"What are you doing?" says the cook.

"Your shelves are overflowing," I tell her. "Look!" I trot over to the pantry door and push it open. "There are people in the village who could do with some this. Can we take it, help them out?"

She stares at me, open-mouthed. "But you said. . ."

Bella explodes. "Don't you realize what is happening here? The Judge is a crook! He's a thief, a villain, a cheat, a fraud!"

The cook looks horrified for a moment, her eyes widen with horror. Then, without warning she shrieks. "Mister Widdrington!" she screams. "Mister Widdrington!"

Bella grabs the baskets and swings them off the table. She passes one to me. Then she plucks an apple from the top of hers and walks calmly over to the cook.

"Mister Widd—"

Bella stuffs the apple into the cook's mouth. "Something for the needy," she says. "Good afternoon." Then she swings round and marches back the way we came.

But standing outside the side door, a riding crop gripped firmly in his gloved hand, is a newly wigged Judge Butterworth, a stony-faced son at each shoulder.

"Well, well, well," he says, recognizing us instantly. "The horse thieves of Idlegreen."

THIRTY-EIGHT

We're led through the house, Butterworth wobbling in front of us, his sons behind. The Judge's long yellow silk jacket makes a slight squeaking noise, like arguing mice. His sons are silent but they smell of ash and damp air. "Don't think I'm taking you on a tour of the house," he says without looking round. "But I think you should realize exactly who you are dealing with."

He leads us into the hallway, past the clock, into a large bright room. I can hear Bella gasp, but whether it's a gasp of admiration or of rage, I can't tell.

The room is huge. The walls are wood panelled and white, and decorated with huge, dark paintings of horses and still landscapes. There are two enormous fireplaces, neither of them lit, and above these, on broad mantelpieces, are bright, ornate candlesticks. There are large white armchairs and sofas, hidden beneath fat cushions. Glass chandeliers throw diamonds of muted light across the ceiling. Nothing looks damaged, or even slightly dusty. Butterworth's vast wealth has survived intact.

At the far end of the room is a musical instrument, not a piano, but similar; it looks hundreds of years old and is probably priceless. I can't imagine the Judge's stubby little fingers playing anything more than "Three Blind Mice" on it.

Butterworth moves towards one of the windows that opens out on to a balcony. "Come on," he booms, "this isn't for your amusement. You need to understand a few things before you both get locked up."

I glance at Bella, who just seems to shrug. We follow the Judge on to the balcony. It's larger than I expected. In one corner is a table, a large bowl of fruit in the middle. In the centre of the balcony is a large cylinder of brass set on a tripod. I know what this is, it's his telescope.

The door behind is shut and, glimpsing back, I see Butterworth's sons looking through the glass at us. The Judge waddles over to the table and removes an apple from the bowl. He takes a gargantuan bite of the apple, and crunches it noisily.

"My own apples," he says. "Sell very well, you

know. Like everything else we produce here. You see, I'm not a farmer, I'm a businessman. Farmers just grow things, I produce things: fruit juices, cider, pickles and pies. I manufacture and package and export. I am rich and successful and my achievements are not an accident."

"You're a thief," I say, without thinking.

"You stole ash from the Green," Bella adds.

"You took it last night, and your family probably took it last time, it's obvious."

Judge Butterworth ignores us. "Look at my telescope!" he says, as if he were a children's conjurer who had just produced this thing from a box of tricks. "I watch you, I watch Blight, watch the ash wardens as they take a deposit to the bank or bring me some fresh stuff to lay down, not that I'll have much need to do that for a long time."

"And the comet," I add, "watch that as well, did you?"

"Of course, I'm a keen astronomer. The clocks, and of course the famous prophecy, they were supposed to be a warning, but they became a sort of promise of riches to come." His face suddenly loses its relaxed expression. "Now, what I want you to see is this." He ushers us forward to the telescope, pushes me towards the eyepiece. "Look now, but don't touch."

I have to lift myself up on my toes and close one eye, and it isn't easy. Eventually the circle of blurred light begins to make sense. There's a wagon coming along the lane, just behind Blight's Tor, close to the point we had the accident.

Butterworth pulls me away and pushes Bella to the telescope. "Here comes Sergeant Smedley in the prison wagon. He will be returning with you to Hook Head. You'll have a few other passengers, six of my ash wardens, to accompany you. I sent for him about an hour ago, when I saw you crossing the Green." He pauses here and rubs his hands together. "I know everything that goes on here, and you two are just annoying little grubs. I look down on your tiny little house, and although I'm so sorry about what happened to the roof, perhaps I'll get a better view of what little creatures do inside their poky nests."

Then he bends towards me and his eyes are bulging.

"You need to be squashed!"

He plunges a fist through the air until it slams into his other palm.

He pushes his bulk in front of the telescope. "They'll be here in ten minutes. And you'll be taken away from here, locked up."

I feel my blood thumping in my head. "We'll

fight back, Butterworth," I tell him through my teeth. "I mean it, I know we will get you, sooner than you think."

"Oh yes, I forgot," he points his stubby finger at me. "You were the destiny of Idlegreen – the one who can predict the future!" And then he throws back his wigged head and roars. "Well, tell me this, then, great prognosticator, how long will it be before your thieving father attempts to rescue you? Because when we've got all of you, then your troubles will really start."

He turns back to the telescope and shifts its position. He points it over the Green, over the tor where Frank Broadfoot lives. I notice how much darker the sky is now and how low and heavy it seems. At that moment a thick drop of rain falls on my hand.

"Would you like to see your new home?" Again he pushes me to the eyepiece. I'm looking at a bleak island out at sea. "That is Gull Rock. Upon it there's a little prison. There are three cells. One each. No cell doors, no bars, just the cold sea. Not inhabited at the moment, hasn't been for a few years. I won't ask you to guess where it got its name. You'll enjoy your diet of cormorants' eggs, seaweed and rainwater. For as long as I feel you deserve."

I pull away and Bella steps back, refusing to look. Another drop of rain thuds on to the balcony just in front of me, exploding like a ripe fruit. Butterworth doesn't notice. He nods towards the windows.

His sons step out towards us. They look tense and watchful, just in case one of us makes a bid for freedom. My arms are grabbed and I'm pushed back into the white room. Bella gets the same treatment; I can hear her hissing something under her breath. She stumbles as she's shoved forward.

"Say hello to Mitchell for me, will you?" shouts Butterworth from behind us. We don't respond. "He was the last guest on Gull Rock. Although I suppose he's been dead about three years now. You'll recognize him easily. His skull is probably the one with the most hair."

And as we're pushed away I hear Butterworth's laughter echo into the house, making the strings on the instrument in the corner buzz and vibrate like a box full of angry bees.

THiRTY-NiNE

Old Wolfgang is seated at the reins of the prison wagon and looks extremely grim. Sergeant Smedley is standing next to it, as well groomed as I remember him. "Come along, you two," he says without malice. "Let's get you back to the Head."

Behind him the lead-grey sky, beginning to bulge like an old hammock, is full of electricity.

"Now, if you don't mind, I'd like to chain you two together. Only one pair of cuffs, you see." We obligingly hold out our arms, helpfully lined up next to each other ready for him. The policeman nods to the Butterworth boys, who don't wait to see us off. Smedley reaches into the open wagon and pulls out a box that he places on the ground as a step. We climb aboard.

A large raindrop hits the top of the sergeant's helmet. It makes a faint popping sound that makes him turn to look, but he doesn't recognize what it is. I hear Bella stifle a snort.

Then another raindrop, this one as big as a

grape, splatters into the dust on the floor of the cart. The mark it leaves is the size of a fried egg.

Wolfgang gives a shout and the wagon rolls forward.

Sergeant Smedley is watching us. But his stare is more like a grandfather than a prison warden. He looks sorry for us. "Are you comfortable?" he asks. "Not too tight, are they, those cuffs?"

"No, they're fine, thank you," I answer. I lean towards Bella, then, pretending to look back over my shoulder, I whisper in her ear, "Deep down I think Smedley's on our side."

Bella's eyes brighten up. She shifts towards the sergeant and asks, "Actually, I wonder, could you take them off. They are a bit tight."

"I'm sorry, dear," says Smedley, "I promised the Judge I would keep you two chained together. And it would be silly of me to break a promise to the Judge."

"He's the criminal," Bella spits back. "He stole our ash from the Green. He knew exactly what he was doing."

"You should be careful what you say, young lady," says Sergeant Smedley, immediately rising from his seat.

"The man is a crook, sergeant," I tell him. "You realize, don't you, that the ash falling around us is the same stuff that is locked in Butterworth's Bank? That it's the stuff that makes this place so fertile? The Judge took cartloads of it from the Green last night, where most of it fell. Look," I shout, "look, you can see the tracks!"

Sure enough the snaking lines criss-crossing the Green are still there, the evidence of Butterworth's crime.

Smedley scratches his chin. "There's no proof he actually took anything," he says after a pause.

"Then what are they doing?" Bella cries, standing up and pulling me up with her. She points to the side of the tor on which the wardens and Butterworth's labourers are still working, pushing the ash across a wide area of newly ploughed field. "He's getting rid of the evidence as quickly as he can," Bella tells Smedley, sitting down again. "By the time we get to Hook Head he'll have worked the lot of it into his land, or locked it up in his cellars and disguised it as the old ash."

Wolfgang, who has been as careful as possible up until now not to show any interest in what we are saying, brings the horse to a standstill. Standing just outside the gates of Butterworth's mansion, back from their work on the hill, are six red-jacketed ash wardens, their squat, black hats neatly on their heads. Smedley passes them the box and one by one they step up and on to the wagon, bidding him good afternoon and ignoring us.

"Afternoon, Roger," says Smedley and, "Nice to see you again, Angus." He knows each one by name, and they all know him.

One sits either side of Bella and me, the other four settle opposite us. I recognize two of them from their sentry duty outside the stores.

"Working hard this morning?" asks Smedley, innocently.

They all sigh. Roger removes his hat and mops his brow. "Up all night taking the stuff off the Green," he says. "And then the boss is telling us we have to get it all raked in. Very eager he was." The wagon moves off again, along the lane that circles the Green.

"We're grateful that you needed an escort," says Angus. "Otherwise we'd be up there until midnight the way things are going."

Angus, Roger and the others look tired and even older. Their faces are lined and weary. They look exhausted. Smedley is studying them with his eyes narrowed. He realizes our story is true.

"What's Gull Rock like?" I ask.

Sergeant Smedley sits up suddenly.

One of the older ash wardens laughs. "Place

where the villains used to be banished. Transported to the rock and left to fend for themselves. Sort of capital punishment, really."

"The Judge said that's where we'd be going once my father turned up," I tell them.

"Then hope your father never turns up," laughs the old warden.

Several drops of rain fall, hitting shoulders, backs and the wagon floor.

"Looks like the heavens are about to open," says Sergeant Smedley. "Sorry there's no canvas, boys."

There is a sudden flash of pearl-white light, revealing the innards of clouds. Thunder follows, booming across the tors, bouncing back, then it rolls across the floor of the island like an enormous, invisible bowling ball.

Rain comes down, heavy, thick globules of the stuff. And I can see now that the rain is full of dust, and the grains burst from their watery prisons when a drop hits the floor. In seconds the floor of the wagon is awash, and rainwater is sloshing about our feet. The wheels of the wagon are flinging up wet soil, as well as the rain that falls on their spokes. It comes from everywhere, and pours down our faces; it's in our eyes and mouths and soon gets into our clothes. Although there is no wind, the rain is so fierce and so intense it hurts. The pony is beginning to slow and the rhythm of its movement is broken.

Wolfgang, his face dripping and his clothes already dark with wet, turns and shouts at us through the noise. "This isn't going to stop soon."

Smedley looks from face to face. He knows any decision rests with him. The rain explodes around him. It's everywhere; it's almost a battle now. "Let's keep going," he shouts back to Wolfgang, at last. "No point in stopping, is there?"

I feel the wagon make a turn and realize we are beginning to climb. It's the lane where Wolfgang crashed before, where I was flung out. I try to look ahead but the rain is clawing my face. I can see the lane rising ahead of us, grey and shining and moving. It's no longer a lane, it's a cascade, a tumbling gush of water, bringing earth and ash and anything else that it can sweep into its course.

The wagon suddenly begins to slide and the horse loses its footing. It stumbles backwards and we are thrown violently sideways.

One of the ash wardens slips off the bench and splashes on to the floor of the wagon and remains on all fours, panting like a dog. "My knee," I hear him say.

Sergeant Smedley tries to help the old man up

but then there is another sudden movement of the wagon and the policeman falls too, landing awkwardly on his elbow. His yelp and the way he holds himself suggest he's hurt. The two of them are now almost swimming about on the floor of the wagon. Bella reaches out with her free hand and the sergeant takes it. He nods his thanks to her but still can't get up.

The wagon begins slipping back further. The horse is frightened; I can see its eyes, white and alarmed.

"OK, that's it," shouts Wolfgang, swivelling to look back at us. He pulls hard on the reins to bring the horse round, but it shakes and ducks and bobs its head.

Sergeant Smedley manages to pull himself up but he is grimacing in pain. The old ash warden is helped up now, and looks pale and disorientated.

The air explodes with light, there is an enormous crash of thunder and the rain becomes more intense, becomes heavier and noisier.

Wolfgang jumps off his seat and the next time I see him he's grabbed the horse by the bridle at its jaw and is leading it round. The wagon seems to rotate until we're gently rolling or sliding, it's hard to tell which, back down the hill.

Then Bella is standing and yelling at Wolfgang.

She has my arm locked to hers and both arms are flapping about, trying to tell him something. Wolfgang seems to understand her. And, after a minute or two, so do I.

Wolfgang jumps back up and takes the reins and now we're on level ground the horse is brought under control.

We're heading across the Green, back towards the stores.

We may still have a chance.

FORTY

The kitchen is warm and dry and full of drenched bodies. Red jackets hang above the stove along with the sergeant's uniform and a line of black hats sits on a shelf above. Elizabeth has bandaged Smedley's elbow and now he sits at the table wearing her pink dressing gown. Wolfgang stands in the doorway, a little uneasy, concerned, he explains, about the pony he's left tied up outside. Above us the rain beats down, not as heavy now, but still loud.

Elizabeth hands out soup, cake, biscuits, tea, whatever anyone wants. The ash wardens have heaped plates and relieved faces. In their damp cotton vests they look small and frail but all very grateful.

Sergeant Smedley has removed the handcuffs and as I have no change of clothes I am allowed to stand by the stove, turning slowly to dry myself. Bella disappears for a few minutes and when she returns she is wearing a summer dress decorated with prints of flowers and fruit. She looks beautiful. When the wardens see her, their eyes light up.

"Oswald," she says to me in a resolute voice, "I think it's time to get the bank notes." She knew about the paper money I was working on, but I didn't think she was very impressed. "Have you forgotten already?" she says. "You were designing them earlier. Go and get them!"

I push a biscuit into my mouth and squeeze past Wolfgang, through the stockroom into the stores. The floor is flooded and rain is pouring through the roof. I go to the till and grab the sheets I left there.

When I return to the kitchen Bella has everyone's full attention.

"Oswald wants to start his own bank," she says. Then she looks at me with a smile on her face that signals I should explain.

"We're offering you all a chance of a lifetime," I tell them. "And you don't have to accept or refuse now. When your jackets are dry you just put these into your pockets and make up your minds later. If you don't want to take up the offer, you just rip them up." I hold up the sheaf of my hand-drawn bank notes.

The wardens are confused, so is Elizabeth.

"Mum," says Bella, "sign these, please." Elizabeth looks at the sheets for a few seconds and seems to understand. Bella passes her mother a pen and, after I have cut the paper into several strips, each one identical, Elizabeth signs them and they are handed around, one for Smedley, one for each of the wardens, and one for Wolfgang.

Each of them examines the strips of paper carefully. One or two of them smile and point out the carefully drawn butterflies and the picture of the stores.

Bank of Idlegreen
I promise to pay the bearer the sum of
50 pots of new Idlegreen ash
signed
Elizabeth Evans

"The Green belonged to my mother, and has been owned by my family for generations," says Elizabeth. "Therefore the ash that fell last night is ours."

The wardens stare up at her.

"And if you want it, it's yours too," I tell them. "There's one of those bank notes for each warden that joins us."

"You won't get the ash back from the Judge," says Roger. "He will kill rather than hand it over."

"Well, if you're with us, we can try," Bella says.

Sergeant Smedley shakes his head. "You are fine people," he says. "Good people. But the Judge is powerful. He is the master of the island." Then his expression changes. "But, if he has committed a crime, he should be brought to justice." The ash wardens nod solemnly. And then the sergeant sneezes and everyone jumps. Elizabeth passes him a handkerchief. He thanks her and continues. "But how we do that is beyond me."

The wardens sit in silence now, clutching the new currency of the Bank of Idlegreen. On those pieces of paper is a guarantee of enough ash for them to live in comfort for the rest of their lives.

Elizabeth disappears for a moment and returns with a tin whistle. I glance towards Bella, expecting her to roll her eyes at her mother's eccentricity. But when Elizabeth produces a melody more suited to a day filled with warmth and sunshine, Bella, who looks like that summer day to come, claps her hands and in the tiny space available to her, begins to dance.

Then Elizabeth sings, and the wardens join in. It's not a song I know, but I am soon able to follow, clapping my hands and stamping my feet.

Angus sings a long, melancholy solo, and

everyone listens in silence, and the rain still falls, beating a tricky rhythm on the roof.

Sergeant Smedley tells the story of the day of Dad's arrest and his surprise when he discovered Bella and Elizabeth were prepared to look after me.

"We're not cousins, you know, sergeant," I admit. "My father made all that up."

Smedley nods, as if it should be expected.

I tell the story of our rescue from the sea, of the basking shark and of our escapes and exploits on Greater Fury and the other islands. The wardens listen intently, some of them shaking their heads at my father's unscrupulous ways. But I feel their sympathy grow, especially when I tell them about the day Mum died and we had to leave the city to make a living.

Elizabeth picks up where she left off, lifting the mood with another jaunty tune. The wardens nod their heads to the beat, or tap their toes. Above us, the rain begins to ease off.

When the clothes are dry and stomachs are full, the red jackets are slipped back on and the black hats are pulled down on dry scalps. The sergeant buttons his jacket and slips the chinstrap of his helmet into position.

"Right," says Smedley. "I must ask you, Oswald

and Bella, to remain in the vicinity of the Green until I receive further instructions."

"So, we're not going back to Hook Head today?" Bella asks.

"That will not be possible," says the sergeant. "And, anyway, I think we have some other business to attend to."

Realizing everyone is ready, Wolfgang turns and leads us out. But once we're on the lane, we stand and stare in utter disbelief. All eyes are on the same thing.

We have stepped into a very different world.

FORTY-ONE

Above the Green, the sky is clearing and there are even patches of blue. The clouds are all but spent and are dispersing. The air tastes clean, free from dust and ash.

Bella, in her summer dress and heavy boots, is the first to break from the trance and walk across the lane. As she steps on to the Green a brushstroke of sunlight travels over her and moves quickly across the island. She turns and looks at us. She can't believe what she sees, and nor can any of us. I notice Roger clasp his bank note tightly in his hand.

The rain has been falling heavily most of the afternoon and now, in the early hours of the evening, as the darkness and the dust is rinsed away, we realize the Green is not what it was.

Nor is Butterworth Tor. Almost all of one side of the Judge's hill has collapsed. It has become a huge river of ash and mud and slipped down into the bowl of the island and filled it. The elegance and majesty of Butterworth Tor is reduced to a soggy, muddy quarry. Several of the outbuildings have disappeared and the Judge's mansion sits precariously on the edge of a vast, ugly hollow. The Green has reclaimed what was always its own. The ash is back where it belongs.

And that is not all. Looking across we can see how the same thing has happened to Blight's land, although not to such a drastic extent. His soil, too, has been washed down, along with several trees that have been uprooted and lie on the lane that separates his property from the Green.

High up on Butterworth Tor, we can make out a round, yellow-suited figure climbing on to his horse. It's Judge Butterworth. He seems to be riding in circles, possibly calling out for his workforce, who, before the rain, were there to take his commands, but who now must have disappeared into barns and outhouses and are probably not in a hurry to make an appearance.

"Well, well, well," says Sergeant Smedley at last. "This is a very interesting situation."

And now the Judge is galloping down the drive towards the main gates. He is on his way.

"Gentlemen," announces Sergeant Smedley, "you are all aware that the Green is the rightful property of Mrs Evans, here."

There are murmurs and mutterings, all of which, more or less amount to agreement.

"If you are, and I cannot see how you cannot be, then you must also agree that any attempt to remove anything from here is a criminal act and is therefore an arrestable offence."

"I agree!" shouts Roger. "Without a doubt."

"Prepare yourselves, then," says the sergeant. "Here comes His Lordship."

Butterworth's horse circles the perimeter of the Green. It leaps broken branches and the remains of the fallen trees. As our eyes follow him we notice another shambling figure, this one on foot, heading towards us. It's Hugh Blight.

I move between the ash wardens, repeating the same thing in a whisper to each of them.

"Remember, the bank notes you are holding are a guarantee, a promise. You each have a share in this now. I am sure Sergeant Smedley will be a witness to that."

The wardens follow Butterworth's progress around the Green, but now and again cast their eyes down to examine their strips of paper.

Now we can hear Hugh Blight. His voice is

loud and angry. His words are carried on a sudden warm breeze. "Thieves!" he is yelling. "You stinking thieves!"

Sergeant Smedley straightens himself up. He fiddles with his moustache. I can tell from where I am standing that he thinks this is definitely not the way to speak to a policeman.

And then Butterworth's horse, snorting and stamping, is brought to a standstill before us. The Judge glares down at the ash wardens before turning his anger towards Sergeant Smedley.

"You, man, what in blazes do you think you are doing? Why do these children still remain at liberty? Why are they not even handcuffed?" His face is swollen with anger, his eyes almost popping out of their sockets. "You are a dunce, man!" the Judge hollers. "A buffoon, a clown, an idiot! I relieve you of all your duties! Now, you," Butterworth turns his anger on the ash wardens. "Get over to the farm and get the wagons out. Start shifting this stuff."

It's my turn to speak. "I think they'll need about three hundred years," I say. "Can't you just wait until the comet comes round again? Perhaps it'll fall on some of your land next time, Mister Butterworth."

The landslide has brought more than just the

ash the Judge had carted away last night. And he knows that. He's lost much more than he took from us. His lips curl into a snarl.

"Is nobody here going to do as I say?"

And then Hugh Blight arrives. He looks wild, as if he hasn't slept all night. His clothes are damp, creased and crumpled. "My farm!" he croaks, wiping his face with a cuff. He looks across at the Green, and then back up to his tor. "My farm has been stolen!"

There are a few suffocated laughs from some of the ash wardens. Judge Butterworth's glare cannot quieten them now.

"Your Honour," says Blight, pointing at Elizabeth from beside the Judge's horse, "that woman has stolen my farm!"

A loud "Ha!" explodes from Bella's mouth. "Yes," she says, "we carried it off in the night!"

"Do not be so insolent, child!" roars the Judge. Bella responds perfectly. She pokes her tongue out. "How dare you ridicule me! How dare you!" The Judge is bloated with rage. He looks dangerous.

Then we realize someone is calling out to us from behind the remains of the stores. The Judge shifts in his saddle to get a better view. Sergeant Smedley, the wardens and Elizabeth move round to the side of the building where the path is visible.

"Good evening, everyone!" a deep, jaunty voice pronounces. Immediately, I know it's Frank Broadfoot. But when he appears I realize he's not alone.

"You!" booms the Judge.

It's Dad.

He limps out from the side of the stores, his sun-pinked face beaming with delight. A young man with long black hair and a wide smile supports him.

"Warm hours, fellows!" Dad grins, waving his hands in the air and jumping from foot to foot. His beard looks longer, more pointed and very orange. His hair is pulled back and tied into a ponytail. He is dressed in nothing that I recognize and has transformed himself into one of the bark riders. I notice he has a knee strapped up. "Oswald!" he cries, and limps towards me, arms outstretched. He picks me up, swings me round and drops me down again. "It's so good to see you again," he whispers. He gestures to his fellow bark rider. "Tyrone," he says, "come and meet my son."

"Rocky's had a bit of an accident," says Tyrone. "But he was determined to get back here."

Dad has found himself a new friend, and a new name.

The Judge is looking from Dad to me, from Tyrone to Frank Broadfoot and back to Dad. "Smedley, isn't that the fugitive?"

Sergeant Smedley's gaze wanders lazily across to Dad. He doesn't want to appear too eager to help the Judge. "Don't recognize him," says Smedley. "What did you say his name was?"

"It's Rocky," replies Tyrone.

"Not the same man," announces Smedley. "Nothing like him."

Frank Broadfoot roars with laughter. "A case of mistaken identity, Your Honour. Case dismissed."

The Judge's eyes narrow and his neck seems to inflate. He doesn't know what to say.

"Arrest the woman!" snaps Hugh Blight. He looks up at the Judge, his face almost pleading with him.

"Shut up you idiot!" Butterworth snarls.

I step forward and address the ash wardens. "Gentlemen," I tell them, "as partners in our new business, I hope you will ensure the Green is free of trespassers. The land will not flourish if the lazy and greedy are allowed to help themselves." I take a step to one side and pass Frank Broadfoot one of the bank notes from the few I have remaining still clutched in my hand. "A present for you," I tell him. "Thank you for your help."

He stares down at the strip of paper and, for a few seconds, seems to think it's a joke. But when he looks up and sees Sergeant Smedley and the ash wardens watching him, waving their notes in the air, like little flags, he smiles at me and winks.

When Butterworth sees this he stands up on his stirrups to try and get a better view. He wants to see what everyone is holding. He soon begins to rant. "It's what I say that matters around here, not a child, not a boy who pretends to see into the future. Not a girl who can't even run a shop! I am the law here. I say what is right and what is wrong. Smedley!" he yells. "Smedley, arrest everyone! Everyone, do you hear me? You are all charged with conspiracy."

Smedley stares at the Judge, but makes no movement.

The Judge looks confused. Suddenly all his power, and nearly all his wealth, have evaporated. He kicks at his horse, pulls at the reins and, with a thunder of hooves, is propelled back towards the remains of his farm.

Hugh Blight, realizing his only ally has deserted him, turns and runs.

And now the sun breaks through the last

fragments of cloud and the skies above the Green are summer blue. A red admiral flutters past, dipping and bobbing.

"You see," says Dad, "I told you everything would work out in the end."

FORTY-TWO

Wolfgang was delighted to help us take the first cartload of ash to the newly opened Bank of Idlegreen at Hook Head. The first consignment came to one hundred and twenty pots, and that was just the beginning.

The wardens, Sergeant Smedley and Frank Broadfoot received their share and even when all that was done, they made it clear they wanted to stay and help us get the Green and the stores set up for the year.

Bella and I sit outside on the lane, listening to the roofers banging and shouting. Occasionally they stop for a drink or a sandwich, but otherwise they keep at it ten hours a day, putting the place back together.

We know Butterworth is watching us and now and then we give him a wave. Perhaps he is planning something, but if he is, it'll take everything he has to persuade his few remaining staff to turn against us. All the ash wardens have deserted him and joined our new bank; they could see the Judge's reign of terror had come to an end.

There are still hundreds of pots of ash to be carted away and, until that is done, we have to keep watch on the Judge. But the wardens are keen to help us protect what is now ours. As well as their fifty pots each, they get one for every week they stay with us. That's what the Judge gave them for a year's hard labour.

I'm pretty sure that Butterworth won't ever be able to lure them back into his service. They've all realized what a crook he is. And when we told them he planned to send us to Gull Rock, they were appalled.

Dad is inside with Elizabeth, helping her redecorate. They have plans to buy a boat, to sail to the mainland and buy some new furniture, maybe even a clock for the kitchen.

Dad is calmer now, and is enjoying his new life. He listens to what everyone else has to say, and hasn't mentioned Mother Fortune for several weeks. Whenever we discuss our adventures he seems embarrassed, and a little uncomfortable. It's a good sign. I think he's getting better.

There are plans to divide the Green into three. At the far end, beneath the sand dunes, we'll plant fruit trees. In the middle we'll grow wheat and maybe some corn. And then they'll be some sort of public park, with trees and flowers and statues and a bandstand.

Bella and I have been trying to work out the history of the Green. The clocks must have been made when the memory of the last comet was still clear. Maybe they were designed for future generations, maybe they were just dedicated to the comet, a sort of tribute.

We still look after the clocks, well, ten of them anyway. All have survived intact. We know the Judge has one, and there surely is a twelfth, standing in the crooked house on the top of Blight Tor.

Dryden, too, has received a small share in our new wealth. The Clackers knew that Blight and Butterworth were waiting for the moment the clocks would predict the fall of the comet. Both of them gave Mrs Clacker a cartload of ash every year, to keep her quiet. Dryden, however, wasn't able to keep the secret. Whenever he looked like he was going to talk, she beat him.

We've made sure the winkle pickers who helped us through the Judge's cordon, and the bark riders who welcomed Dad have received a share in our good fortune.

Butterworth probably knew that when the

comet came there would be panic. He had his little army ready, and Dad was the perfect excuse for their presence. They weren't rounding up a fugitive; they came to take every bit of ash that fell.

And the telescope on the veranda. That wasn't just for watching us. It was for watching the comet, Khoronos, King Curlymane.

The wardens are working now, although I'll have to go over soon and tell them to stop. They have to make sure the surplus ash is removed and potted and the rest ploughed and spread to thicken the thin soil beneath. Then the planting will start. In a few months the first harvest will come. We'll fill the shelves of the stores, and the villagers can come and help themselves. We'll send some produce to Hook Head, and, once every month or so, a boat full of our goods will journey to the mainland and the other islands.

We have quite a future ahead of us.

Bella wants to turn the stores into a hotel, but there isn't much point. We won't need the money.

"It's not the money," she tells me, "it's the thought of telling our guests the story, the tale of Idlegreen and the downfall of Judge Humpty himself."

But I have other ideas. I haven't told her yet.

Somewhere on the Green, perhaps on the far side of the new park, I want to create a huge greenhouse, bigger than the Judge's mansion, bigger than the whole of Hook Head. Inside I want to grow as many different plants as possible, especially cabbages and big green-leafed vegetables, nettles and milk parsley. And spectacular flowers, ones that will be taller than me, with petals the size of my hand, of bright orange and yellow. I'll grow them, not because I want to look at them, or because I want to show them to anyone. The flowers will be resting places, where they'll stay long enough for me to study the thousand reflections in their compound eyes, or see their antennae twitch. There will be no pins or mounting board and the windows and doors will be left open for them to come and go.

Children will arrive with their mums and dads from Hook Head and I'll be able to give them guided tours, point out the purple emperors and the swallowtails, watch the toddlers giggle and stare in astonishment as a red admiral or a brimstone lands on an outstretched hand, then crawls to their fingertips and, after scenting the air, rises up into the airy dome, the glass sanctuary that will be a butterfly haven, the new Museum of Idlegreen.